THE SLEEPING
BRIDE

Further Titles by Dorothy Eden from Severn House

BRIDE BY CANDLELIGHT
THE DEADLY TRAVELLERS
LET US PREY
THE PRETTY ONES
THE SCHOOLMASTERS DAUGHTER
THE SLEEPING BRIDE

THE SLEEPING BRIDE

Dorothy Eden

This edition published in Great Britain 1995 by
SEVERN HOUSE PUBLISHERS LTD of
9–15 High Street, Sutton, Surrey SM1 1DF.
Originally published 1959 by Macdonald & Co. Ltd.
This first hardcover edition published in the USA 1996 by
SEVERN HOUSE PUBLISHERS INC of
595 Madison Avenue, New York, NY 10022.

British Library Cataloguing in Publication Data
Eden, Dorothy
  Sleeping Bride. – New ed
  I. Title
  823 [F]

  ISBN 0-7278-4843-7

Typeset by Hewer Text Composition Services, Edinburgh.
Printed and bound in Great Britain by
Hartnolls Ltd, Bodmin, Cornwall.

1

It was quite late when the car, a sleek Jaguar, stopped at the café on the Portsmouth Road.

It was a makeshift café, merely a caravan with the side let down to expose the counter on which stood thick white cups, some of them still holding dregs of tea. Under a glass dome was a plate with a melancholy array of cakes.

The proprietor was elderly and a little short-sighted. He appeared from behind the counter where he had been reading a paper-backed Homer (he was something of a philosopher), and said, "What would you like?" Peering at his customer, he added a belated, "Sir."

"Two cups of tea, please. I want to take them to the car." The man smiled suddenly, with great charm. "My aunt is elderly and not very well."

"That's all right, sir. Milk and sugar?"

The customer had to go over to the car to ask. A clear-carrying voice answered.

"Milk and sugar for Aunt Blandina, thank you. No sugar for me."

The café proprietor was a little ashamed then that he did not provide such amenities as saucers. But these were not his usual customers. Lorry drivers, youths on bicycles, motor cyclists, stopped and leaned on the counter to drink their tea. But it was not often an expensive car, with this kind of customer, stopped.

As an unusual gesture of service he went over to the car presently to collect the cups. He saw the occupants, a good-looking dark girl and an old woman dressed in black with nicely waved white hair and several heavy rings on her fingers.

She looked a well-cared-for old lady, plump and pink-cheeked. But it was her eyes which had a bewildered, lost look that he observed particularly.

So that was the trouble. It was not undue weakness in her legs but in her head that had made the polite nephew keep her in the car.

"I think she's feeling better now, Armand," he heard the girl saying as the man got back into the car. "Aren't you, Aunt Blandina?"

"Yes, dear. Much better, thank you." The thin, wavery voice caught the café proprietor's attention. "But I wish I knew where we were going. I don't know this road at all." She looked out of the car window as if she were seeing the dusk-dark landscape, the strips of cloud following a rising moon, the isolated lights shining in houses, and the long straight road, faintly gleaming, for the first time. And as if it were something seen in a half sleep, or a nightmare. "It's a strange road," said her anxious voice. "So strange. . . ."

It was two months after that evening that Aurora, the dark-haired girl, made ready to begin another journey. And this was not just a trip by car into the country. This was to be much longer, and quite final.

She had come to her decision with the greatest difficulty. Shock, suspicion, fear, and also, to be quite honest, a pleased appreciation of Philip Nash's admiration for her all came into it.

She had not meant to let the tall casual stranger, with that intense awareness beneath his air of languor, take her seriously. Nor had she dreamed that he would begin to do so. He was merely a wandering artist (as in mediæval days he might have been a strolling player) who, back from the tropics, suddenly had a desire to paint the pale pure face of an English beauty, as a contrast to the chocolate forms his brush had been occupied with over the past few months. His direct approach to her in a coffee bar had been amusing and flattering. She would not have believed then that in a month she would have arranged to marry him.

6

But neither would she have believed some other things, much more startling and incredible. She would not let her mind dwell on those as she did her rather hasty packing.

It had been her plan, as soon as she had made her private decision to lead Philip to a proposal of marriage, to have that marriage performed as quickly as possible. When he became unexpectedly conventional about families and observing the usual courtesies she had had to get in touch with her alienated and more or less discarded family and suggest returning to the fold.

But that, too, eventually, began to seem a very good idea. It gave her a feeling of security and protection which at the moment she badly needed. It was a refuge. And also it made just so many more reasons why she couldn't change her mind, which she was so foolishly and dangerously tempted to do.

Besides, it would be nice to see Lydia, her young step-sister, again.

So she gave her flat a sketchy tidying up, preparatory to hers and Philip's return from their honeymoon some weeks hence, and completed her packing. She had done the wisest thing. Everything would work out very well. And safely. . . .

Having said her farewells at the office that morning she had meant to wait until Philip's return from Northumberland where he was visiting relatives. His train was due in the early afternoon.

But after listening to the footsteps on the stairs she couldn't bear to stay in the flat any longer. She had heard them so distinctly on the stone steps, the slow approach, the shuffling outside her door.

If it were that old woman again she couldn't bear it. She wouldn't open the door. She would stand not breathing in the tiny hall, listening to the long imperative ringing of the bell, then the rapping, and the scuffling in the letter-box. She had done this once before, and it had seemed that the old creature would never go away.

This time, however, the footsteps miraculously passed her door and went on laboriously up the next flight of stairs. Aurora sighed with relief. It had been someone else.

7

Neverthless, now she couldn't linger. She was full of apprehension. Finally, tense and jittery, she rang to leave a message at Philip's rooms saying that she would look for him at Waterloo station at three o'clock, and if he were not there then he could follow her down on a later train. That meant that if he arrived back in London in time he could go straight to Waterloo.

He might think her odd, rushing off like this, but he didn't know how imperative it was.

There were no more footsteps, but the telephone rang just as she was closing the last suitcase. She jumped convulsively, then looked uncertainly and with apprehension at the inanimate instrument that emitted such a noise.

Should she answer it? Or should she just go? After all, had it not been for June Birch, her neighbour in the flat below, dropping in with final good wishes just after lunch she would have been gone by now, and the telephone would have been ringing in the empty flat.

She stood there, a slight, dark girl, hugging her arms round herself, her face expressing doubt and fearful eagerness.

The telephone went on ringing.

Why, it would be Philip, of course. How was it that he always came into her thoughts second? That was a fine omen for their marriage.

He probably wanted to tell her that he had got her note, and to arrange where to meet on Waterloo station.

She picked up the receiver with a flourish.

But it was not Philip after all.

"Oh, it's you!" Her face tightened. "I told you not to ring." Refusing to listen to the voice hidden persuasively within the receiver, she cried hysterically, "I told you it was no use. I told you!" And she banged the receiver down, cutting off the voice which had dilated her eyes and wrung her face colourless.

Then she was like a whirlwind, carrying her suitcases to the door, banging windows shut, throwing on her coat and giving a last quick smoothing to her hair. Last of all she suddenly thrust her hand under the mattress of her bed, remembering something hidden there, and taking out a newspaper tore it into pieces and flung the pieces into the waste-paper basket.

After that she was ready to leave. There was no porter to these unpretentious flats, so she had to carry her bags down the stairs herself. In the cold, draughty entrance hall, stone-floored, she met June Birch again, returning home with a laden shopping basket.

"Oh, Aurora, dear, you're just going! All by yourself?"

"Philip's going to meet me at Waterloo."

"Oh, well, then—you'll have a lovely wedding in the country. I hope the sun shines. But it never does, does it! I'll be looking forward to you coming back. Send me a post-card and I'll do some shopping for you. Get in the milk and bread."

"That's kind of you, June. Would you? I'll leave you my key. And I'll send you a note later. I've no idea, really, when we'll be back. Now I must fly."

She hoped that stupid little creature, all starry-eyed about a wedding, hadn't seen the tears on her cheeks. But if she had she would misinterpret them. Pre-wedding jitters. She, Aurora Hawkins, behaving like a jittery *jeune fille*!

She got a taxi almost immediately, and in it composed her face, renewing her lipstick and putting powder over the recent damp marks on her cheeks. When she reached Waterloo station and saw Philip's tall head above the crowd, she told herself, she would run towards him, flinging herself into the safety of his arms.

For now he was her safety, and everything was going to be all right. . . .

But Philip was not there. Either he was later than he had expected to be arriving in London, or he had not got her message. She waited ten minutes, watching the clock, filled with such a sensation of panic and urgency that she knew she must catch the next train. As she had not been able to linger in the flat, neither could she linger here.

She would have to go down alone. But first there was one thing she could do. Rush to the pub across the road and buy a bottle of gin. That would be necessary, if she were to face good-humouredly her mother's questions.

And also to drown this awful and unreasonable remorse that was beginning to overwhelm her.

2

Millicent's letter reached Lydia in Paris. Lydia had just lost her job. Teaching English to two exceedingly spoilt and difficult French children was one thing, but having to fight off advances from their father was another. Even the thought of the summer in Paris and visits to all her cherished places did not make this worth while. Besides, the conceited father did not enjoy being rebuffed. He was astonished and angry, particularly that he should have been spurned by such a plain English Miss who should have been flattered and delighted by his attentions, and it was apparent her tenure in the Avenue Matignon house was going to be extremely brief.

So she acted on impulse, as always, and gave notice to the children's mother, the plump and stately Madame Bertrand, and in spite of shrill, indignant protests left the house that day.

She vaguely thought of looking for another job in Paris, but Millicent's letter, arriving just as she was saying her stiff farewells, changed her plans completely.

She could scarcely believe its contents.

"Darling Lydia,

"You must, when you get this letter, arrange to come home immediately, for what do you think has happened, Aurora has written to say she is being married, and wants to come home for her wedding. Needless to say, I am so delighted I can scarcely think coherently. Especially when a wedding, and an immediate one, is involved.

10

"Aurora, the poor pet, says that it's all very well quarrelling with one's step-father and maintaining this hateful hostility when one is living an ordinary life, but when one plans to marry one needs one's family. So she has written asking to be forgiven for her behaviour, which wasn't entirely her fault, as Geoffrey can be difficult, too.

"You can imagine the whirl I am in. The date is to be the soonest possible, Aurora is leaving her job, whatever it was (she gives no information except the address of her flat which is 5 Radlett Lane, N.W.8), and is coming home on Thursday. I've already seen the vicar and arranged about the church. Fortunately there are very few weddings this month, so we have the choice of several days, but Aurora says no guests except the family.

"So, Lydia, dear, you must come home immediately. If your French family won't give you time off you must give up your job. You can get another one easily enough, and why does it have to be in Paris?

"I'm turning out Aurora's room and making it fresh and pretty. Your father is in a state, there is no other way to describe it. Poor darling, he's had a guilt complex about not having been able to get on with Aurora. As if anyone could have. She does have those impossible moods, and she has always resented my marrying your father.

"But now, as you can see, all is forgiven, and we're so happy. Come home at once, please. There is so much to do. But isn't it all heavenly!

"Much love,

"Millicent.

"PS. Aren't I absurd, I haven't told you who Aurora is marrying. She hasn't said much about him, but his name is Philip Nash, and he is just back in England after some long expedition somewhere. He paints pictures, also. So Aurora will have a life of immense variety, which I think should please her. Much love again, and do catch the next plane— or boat if you can't afford to fly, though I'm sure Geoffrey would send your fare if you are short.

"M."

Millicent, her garrulous, kindly and feather-brained step-mother, certainly had the gift of talking on paper, and her written sentences took almost as much interpretation as her vivacious, garbled spoken ones. She was a dear, but entirely exasperating, and it was not altogether surprising that Aurora, contained and uncommunicative, should have found her mother almost as difficult as her stiff and unbending step-father.

Lydia was extremely fond of them both. She understood her father, his rigidity of principle and his intense shyness, and although she had been only a baby when her own mother had died, and twelve years old when her father had decided to re-marry, she had had a sense of gratitude and pleasure at being gathered into Millicent's warm garrulity.

Aurora, her step-sister, three years her senior, Lydia had admired and longed to resemble. Aurora had treated her with occasional indulgence, but mostly with indifference. She had not understood Aurora's resentment at no longer being the whole of her mother's world, but had been increasingly aware of the hostility between Aurora and her father. It clouded the last years of her childhood and her growing up. Finally, when at the age of twenty-one Aurora had said she was leaving home to live in London, and would not be back except perhaps for a brief week-end visit now and then, it was impossible not to feel relief.

"She took after her own father," Millicent had said tearfully. "When he was angry he did these dramatic things. But she'll get over it. She is my daughter, after all, even if I don't understand her."

Aurora wrote occasionally, and several times telephoned. She gave no personal information about herself, and did not keep her promise to make week-end visits. Geoffrey, Lydia realised, was extremely grieved about the whole thing, but said the girl was of age and if she wanted to live her own life, entirely separated from them, they could do nothing about it.

Millicent had to agree, but her sentimental, effusive nature needed an outlet, and she turned to Lydia to express it. The two became devoted. Twisting Lydia's straight hair, Millicent used to say, "You haven't got Aurora's looks, but you're a dear

12

child. And you'll improve. Anyway, beauty only brings trouble."

But no one knew whether or not it was a man to whom Aurora had gone.

Gradually Lydia, busy with her own pursuits, missed Aurora less. She realised that a storm-centre had been removed from the house, and her shock gave place to an intense curiosity as to what Aurora was doing. Some day she would find out.

Now it seemed that the mystery was to be cleared up. It was, as Millicent had said, intensely exciting. Lydia said a silent thank you to M'sieu Bertrand for his methods which had already organised her departure from the Bertrand household, and rushed off to the Gare du Nord to catch the first boat-train.

As Millicent had predicted, she could not afford the air fare, but with her packing done and her departure planned she would be home almost as quickly by channel steamer.

What, she wondered, having a similar after-thought to Millicent's, was this man Aurora intended to marry like?

Lydia arrived in London with some time to spare before catching her train home. She knew what she was going to do. She was going to the address Millicent had given her to see if Aurora were still at her flat. It would be fun to walk in on her and to renew their old relationship without Millicent hovering talkatively over them. What did Aurora look like now? Had she still that dark, exciting beauty? And what would she think of Lydia at twenty-two?

Not a great deal, Lydia reflected, with a complete lack of self-conceit. Even M'sieu Bertrand, with his ardent advances, had indicated that he did not consider her madly beautiful. But M'sieu Bertrand's tastes definitely leaned towards the voluptuous, and Lydia, with her high cheekbones and sparsely-fleshed body, must have represented a pitiable poverty of choice to him. It was really, in retrospect, rather amusing. She would tell Aurora about it when there was time.

If Aurora had not left London yet they could travel down to Lipham together, and catch up on each other's news.

The block of flats in St. John's Wood was not imposing. It looked respectable enough, but shabby. Lydia's eager feet

13

took her up the stone stairs two at a time. What a good thing, she was thinking, that Aurora didn't have to live in these uninspiring surroundings all her life. But one hoped she was there for half an hour longer, at least.

It was too much to hope, apparently, for no one came in answer to Lydia's ring. She was absurdly disappointed.

It didn't matter. Aurora must already be home, and in two or three hours she would see her.

But it would have been such fun to have this private meeting first. In a vague attempt to make herself think the disappointment was not real, Lydia tried the door handle.

To her intense surprise the door opened. It had not been locked.

So Aurora must be here after all!

"Aurora! Can I come in? It's me! Lydia."

She stepped into a miniature hall and listened. There was no sound from within. The living-room was visible through an open doorway. She went in and noticed all the usual signs of the occupier of the flat being absent, the drawn curtains, the vague disorderliness which it hadn't been worth while to tidy after packing, an ashtray full of cigarette ends, a cup containing dregs of tea, a faint film of dust on the table. Also on the table was a newspaper which had been badly torn and which someone had been trying to piece together.

That was strange, Lydia thought, and glanced idly at its name. *The Daily Reporter,* dated the third of April, she noted, and tucked the information away in her mind to ask Aurora later what it had been she was trying to find.

"Aurora," she called again, uncertainly.

The bedroom also was empty. It was a slit of a room, prettily furnished, giving evidence of Aurora's femininity, but also of her absence, for the bed was made up without sheets, and the wardrobe empty of clothes.

In the kitchen it was the same story, neat cupboards, an empty refrigerator, attractive but inexpensive china, gay paint obviously applied by Aurora herself. The whole flat gave clear indication of its owner, a tidy-minded girl living alone and making the best of rather dreary surroundings.

There were only the two rather odd things to remember and comment on, the unlocked door and the torn newspaper on the table.

And a vague feeling of unhappiness.

The last was purely imagination. It came to Lydia only because of her own disappointment at arriving too late to find Aurora home. An empty flat was always strangely forlorn. She would go downstairs and ring the doorbell of the flat immediately below, and see what she could find out.

The woman who answered her ring was youngish, with primrose-coloured hair in curlers and dejected lines in her face. But she grew extremely animated when Lydia introduced herself—other people's lives were obviously of obsessive interest to her—and she probably saw in this reconciliation of Aurora with her family all the ingredients of a novelette.

"Fancy that! You're Aurora's sister! You're not a bit like her, are you?"

"No, I'm not."

"Oh, I don't say you're not nice looking, but Aurora's quite a beauty, isn't she? I always wondered why some man didn't snap her up long ago. I mean, she's twenty-five, isn't she? I was married at nineteen, more fool me! And divorced at twenty-two."

"Look, Mrs.——"

"Birch. June Birch. Call me June."

"Look, June, I went up to see if Aurora were still there——"

"Oh, she's gone. You've missed her. She called goodbye about half an hour ago."

"Then why wasn't the door of her flat locked?"

"Wasn't it? Good gracious! She must have forgotten to lock it. Well, it's understandable, isn't it? Going off to her wedding. She was so excited."

But here, oddly enough, the talkative woman's words lacked conviction, and a brief puzzled look crossed her face. As if she had pondered on Aurora's lack of excitement.

"Well, anyway, dear, there's nothing to worry about. I have the key Aurora left with me. I'm going to do some shopping

15

for her when she's due back from her honeymoon. I'll give it to you and you can tell your sister you locked up."

It was then that the utterly curious feeling came over Lydia that she didn't want to go up to the flat alone. This building was not wildly gay, but it was respectable, and without dark corners or shoddy stairways. It was filled with completely normal sounds, children's voices, a door slamming somewhere, a radio turned too high. Yet the feeling swept over her that this normality was deceptive. The emptiness of Aurora's flat was a lie. It had not been empty at all. Someone had been there watching her as she prowled about. The person who had unlocked the door and who, startled by her arrival, took cover. Where? Behind the bathroom door, perhaps, or behind the curtains in the living-room.

Oh, nonsense! she told herself. Was she becoming psychic? But if June Birch would come up with her. . . .

"Since the door was unlocked," she said quickly, "I think we ought to make sure everything's all right. I don't know what should be there, but you do."

"Sure, I'll come up with you if you're worrying about burglars," June said good-naturedly. "But it would have to be a pretty slick burglar to find that door open and nip in all in the short time since Aurora left. Come on then, duck."

As they reached the first-floor landing Lydia could hear the telephone ringing in Aurora's flat.

That would startle the intruder, if there were one. She hastily approached the door, expecting every moment to hear the ring cut short as someone lifted the receiver. But the shrill sound continued, and when she turned the door knob ready, with June Birch beside her, to burst in, the door was locked.

It couldn't be! Why, only ten minutes ago she had pulled it shut herself without having a key to turn in the lock. And now, as if she had suffered from an hallucination, it was firmly locked.

Even June, with her worldly air, was startled. "But you said it wasn't locked. Did you try it properly? You must have made a mistake."

16

"I didn't. I went in the flat. I told you. It's been locked since I was here. Just in the last few minutes." A tremor passed over her. "There must have been someone in there all the time."

June's heavily marked eyebrows rose. "Goodness! How queer! Must have been someone Aurora had given a key to. After all—well, I didn't pry, and she didn't talk much. A girl's entitled to privacy."

The telephone inside kept on ringing. Suddenly it was immensely important that it should be answered.

"Open the door," Lydia cried. "Hurry. I want to answer the telephone before it stops ringing."

The telephone was in the tiny hall. Lydia snatched up the receiver while June went past her, warily, into the living-room.

"Hullo!"

"Darling? Is that you? Thank goodness I caught you. I'm running awfully late, and——"

"Just a minute," said Lydia. "This isn't Aurora, if that's who you think you're speaking to."

"Oh! I'm sorry." The voice was deep and attractive. It seemed to vibrate through the receiver. Unconsciously Lydia hugged it closer to her ear. "Who is it, then?"

"It's me. Lydia. The beautiful younger sister."

"I'm pleased to meet you, Lydia. I didn't think that was going to be until this evening. This is Philip Nash speaking. I was trying to catch Aurora. Has she gone?"

"Yes, half an hour ago."

"Then I've missed her. I wanted to tell her I couldn't be at Waterloo the time we planned. I've got held up all round. We were going to have tea before our train left. I'd better fly. I might catch her there now."

"Wait a moment," said Lydia. "I'm coming, too. Where are you ringing from?"

"A call-box in Piccadilly."

"Then wait for me at Waterloo. I'll be about half an hour. If Aurora's there, tell her to wait. We can all go down together."

"Good idea. I'll see you then. And I am pleased to meet you, Lydia."

"I say!" Lydia cried. "Wouldn't it be a good idea to tell me what sort of a person I'm to look for. I'm five feet six, and rather thin, and I'll be wearing a camel-hair coat. My hair is straight and inclined to be sandy, and I'm not, I'll repeat that, I'm not remarkably beautiful."

There was a faint, deep chuckle.

"That's fine, Lydia. Let's leave it. I'll find you."

She put the receiver down very slowly. She had forgotten for a moment that she was standing in Aurora's flat, and that there was a faint mystery about it. She suddenly knew that she was going to find this man, Philip Nash, with the deep, pleasant voice, standing beside Aurora possessively, on Waterloo station, and the thought filled her with the most unreasonable and inexplicable desolation.

"There's no one here," called June Birch from the bedroom. "The place is empty. And nothing's disturbed. As far as I can see, anyway. Whoever was here must have gone down the back stairway." Her voice came nearer. She stood at the door, hands on hips, her pale hair, when its cramping curlers were released, ready to frame a much younger and more hopeful face. "I guess we'd better not be too inquisitive. It's none of our business who might have a key. It could be someone who isn't particularly pleased about Aurora getting married. So perhaps it's a good thing she missed him."

"But there certainly was someone," said Lydia thoughtfully. "Because that newspaper has gone."

"Newspaper?"

"Yes. There was one spread out on the table when I came in before. It had been torn, and then put together again. It's gone now. How very odd!"

18

3

Someone back from the Antarctic, or the headwaters of the Amazon, or the Sahara desert. Lydia looked for a heavy, broad-shouldered young man, sunburnt or windburnt, with rugged features, and likely to possess the deep voice that had vibrated so pleasurably through the telephone.

A hand fell on her shoulder.

"Lydia? The beautiful younger sister?"

She turned and looked into the lean, pale face of an immaculately dressed young man, whose clothes proclaimed Savile Row and whose manners one of the older public schools.

"You can't be Philip!"

"Why not?" His eyes were very blue, and accented by heavy blond eyebrows. He looked deceptively frail, the skin crinkling over his thin cheeks as he smiled.

"But the crocodiles? The desert sunburn or whatever?"

"You mean the dried-up malarial look? I'm sorry. I always stay pink and white like the nicest English debs. Are you disappointed? If it comes to that, you aren't completely what you said yourself."

"How did you know me, then?"

"I don't know. How did I?" He frowned slightly. For a fleeting moment—even then she guessed that the casual merriment would not often be absent—his eyes seemed to go darker. And the tremor that his voice over the telephone had given her went through her again.

"Well, I was right, wasn't I?"

She nodded. She longed, suddenly, for him to say that she was more attractive than she had led him to believe. But he made no comment on her appearance. He was very tall. He was looking down at her. She smoothed her hair, conscious of those very brilliant and perceptive eyes on it.

This was no M'sieu Bertrand with thick lips and fumbling

19

advances. This, she reminded herself quickly, was Philip Nash, her sister's fiancé.

"Aurora's not here?" she asked politely.

"No, I must have missed her. We were to meet at platform 15, but if I couldn't be there in time I was to follow her down. I tried to make it, but everything held me up. I thought she might have got held up, too, and that was why I tried her flat."

"Tried it?"

"Telephoned," he said, eyeing her. "You answered. Don't you remember?"

"Yes, of course. It was just that——"

"What?"

"Oh, nothing." One couldn't tell him about the unlocked door, just supposing the visitor had been, as June Birch suggested, another lover. But was Aurora like that? One didn't know.

"Let's get the tickets and find our train," Philip suggested. "Then you can tell me."

She hoped he would forget the trivial subject. At first it seemed he had. They found an empty compartment, and settled down comfortably, facing one another. Lydia felt cosy and happy, and had forgotten the exhaustion of her journey from Paris. She hadn't yet had the intimate talk with Aurora which was to encompass the lapse of time since they had last met, but Philip, at least, who had known Aurora long enough to want to marry her, could tell her some things.

"I'm staying at the Wheatsheaf," Philip explained. "We decided that would be best, while Aurora fusses with wedding things. I thought at first I was going to escape all that nonsense, but I'm told this is the big day in a girl's life, and she likes her family around."

"Yes," said Lydia uncertainly.

"Oh, you don't need to be cautious. I know all about the suspension of diplomatic relations. A poor show, I thought, and it's high time Aurora went home and had her bottom spanked."

"Then it's because of you that she's gone home?"

20

"No. It was entirely her own idea. But I was all for it. Odd, you know."

"What do you mean?"

His gaze was indolent, but sharp. The exasperating thing was that it gave nothing away. Did he think her very plain? Or was he noticing her appearance at all?

"That she should ignore her young sister, too."

"Oh, I don't suppose she forgot me," Lydia said uneasily. "It was just—well, the argument was with my parents. Daddy isn't the easiest person even as one's father, so as a step-father he's rather worse. And Aurora is pretty quick-tempered and temperamental. Unless she's changed, I expect you've found that out."

"Aurora," he murmured. "The sleeping princess. But she's far from sleeping. Far from it." And then he went back to the awkward subject.

"What was strange about her flat?"

"Strange?"

"You seemed to think I might have been there."

"No, I didn't at all. Actually the tenant downstairs, someone called June Birch, had a key and let me in. There was a torn newspaper on the table. I—I just wondered why Aurora had been trying to put it together."

"We'll ask her when we see her, shall we?" He adjusted the knot of his tie, and brushed a speck of dust from his lapel. "Intriguing," he murmured. "Well, Lydia, what's it going to be like suddenly having a——"

He had been going to say "a brother". She knew he had. But without changing his tone he finished smoothly, "Having your sister restored to you?"

Why had he changed his intended remark? Lydia's heart, to her intense annoyance, and for no good reason, was pounding.

"Is she just as beautiful still?"

He leaned back, his eyes narrowed. "Shall I tell you how I first saw her? Coming into a restaurant off the King's Road. I'd arrived in England that morning, after two years away, mostly in jungles surrounded with dusky beauties, and Aurora

21

was—well, she was her name. I felt as if I'd burst through the thistles and brambles and there she was in front of me, like a goddess."

"Sorry to carp," Lydia said crisply. "But you said a princess a moment ago."

"Princess, goddess," he remained good-humoured. "It doesn't matter. It was raining, and her cheeks were wet and very bright, and she was alone. Gloriously alone. And, most remarkable and wonderful of all, she had no rings on her fingers."

"She'd been asleep for several years," Lydia pointed out, and refused to think of the ring that now sparkled on Aurora's finger.

"Yes. She must have been. That's the only explanation I can think of."

"But you woke her up."

"Yes. I did that, didn't I?" His voice was faintly questioning. Lydia momentarily forgot her sense of desolation and became curious.

"Aren't you sure about it?"

"Well, yes, of course. But a woman has to keep some sense of mystery, hasn't she? She's told me almost nothing about herself."

"Don't you even know where she was working?" Lydia asked, in surprise.

"Oh, yes, for some solicitor in the city. Armand somebody. Armand and his aunts, she used to talk about. He was a Frenchman, I imagine."

"French!" Lydia thought of M'sieu Bertrand, who had unfairly prejudiced her feelings about Frenchmen, and was not surprised that Aurora should have eagerly run to Philip's arms.

Philip was smiling. "You say that just like an English woman from the midlands."

"I've just come back from Paris," Lydia said defensively.

"Have you? What colour are your eyes, Lydia?"

"Can't you see?"

"No. They keep changing. Like water. Or jewels turned to different lights."

Lydia tilted her chin. "Save that for your sleeping princess."

22

"I can't. Black eyes are black all the time. Shall we see if we can find a drink on this train?"

"Are you getting nervous?"

"Lamentably. I've never met in-laws before."

But if he were nervous, Lydia reflected, looking at his fine, austere profile, it was not because of meeting Millicent and Geoffrey. But because of Aurora, and what her feelings were for him.

Or even what his were for her. . . .

4

A wedding in the country. The May trees were out, and the grass green velvet. Two proud and stately swans were followed by cygnets on the pond adjoining the church and the moss-grown churchyard. Ring doves fluttered and cooed about the gables and chimneys of the Wheatsheaf. Cats slept on window-sills in the sun, and children skipped on the cobblestones. The setting was idyllic.

Even Philip had had to admit that. Lydia, half irritated, half amused, had left him at the Wheatsheaf, fussing about the amenities. He said he would be up at the house in time for dinner. He positively must unpack and have a bath and present himself in good order. If Lydia would meantime be the bearer of his respects to her parents and his love to Aurora. . . . When Lydia left him he was leaning his indolent length against the bar, chatting with the bar-keeper, and ordering another double whisky. As if he were indeed nervous. . . .

Millicent flung open the door as soon as she saw Lydia coming up the path.

"My love, here you are! I'm so glad you could come at once. Isn't it all quite wonderful! Aurora arrived an hour ago. She's upstairs resting. She seemed very tired. You didn't happen to see Philip? He was to be on the first train he could catch."

Lydia disentangled herself from Millicent's embrace. "He came down with me. He's at the Wheatsheaf."

"At the Wheatsheaf! But why didn't you bring him here?"

"He wanted to tidy up," Lydia said, and realised how thin an excuse that sounded for a man in love, eager to see his bride's home and his in-laws.

"He's a very meticulous young man. He'll be here to dinner. Don't fuss, Millicent. It's enough that one person is going to fuss at this wedding."

"Who?"

"The bridegroom."

"Lydia, didn't you like him?" Millicent asked in alarm.

Like him? How had she felt about that elegant, irritating young man, seemingly occupied with trivialities, until one caught his brilliant, perspicacious glance?

"I don't know," she said slowly. "I suppose he could be Aurora's type. How does she look, Millicent?"

"Beautiful!" said Millicent ecstatically.

Lydia eyed her, too, with reserve. "I guessed that. I had to listen to Philip on the subject. But what is she really like? Is she happy, do you think?"

Millicent's face, carefully made up and surrounded by perfect, rigid grey curls so that she looked like a plump, pretty doll, was too open for dissembling. Apprehension showed already.

"She tells me nothing! She hasn't changed at all. If I don't ask her questions, that's fine. But if I do, there is that veiled look, instantly! Not exactly hostile. Just 'keep off the grass' sort of thing. With me! Her own mother! Oh, she was perfectly sweet, of course, and to Geoffrey as well. We had tea together. We talked about everything but personal things." Millicent began to tick off on her fingers. "We discussed flowers for the wedding, catering, guests, where she and Philip plan to live, her trousseau, even what we do with poor Mary's kittens nowadays. But as to what she has been doing in the last year, or how much she's in love, or why this rather sudden wedding—nothing! Silence! Utter and complete!"

24

Lydia laughed at the melodrama in Millicent's face. "You can't break the ice all in five minutes, darling."

"I don't think she even likes being home." This Millicent said in a low voice, looking round furtively as if she imagined Aurora might have come silently into the room.

"Oh, nonsense! You can't decide that immediately, either."

"I don't think she is happy, really. When she's not talking, a sort of brooding look comes over her."

"But she's still beautiful."

"Oh, yes. In that haggard, ravished kind of way. I can't think why she hasn't married sooner. Unless she has, of course, and said nothing. How is one to know? Something like that would explain her brooding look."

"Now you're romancing," Lydia chided. "You're aggravated that you don't know about those missing years, so you're making up a story to put in them."

"Perhaps I am. But why is she so mysterious?"

"It's probably an air she's cultivated." Even to the extent of making jigsaw puzzles out of an old page of *The Daily Reporter*, Lydia wondered privately. And to handing out keys of her flat indiscriminately? "When can I see her? Is she asleep now?"

"I don't know. Go up and see. She might talk to you when she won't to me."

Lydia impulsively kissed Millicent on the cheek. "Don't be so sentimental! Here's one daughter, anyway, who's pleased to see you."

"Lydia, darling, you're such a comfort. I adore you. Did you have a nice time in Paris? Was it awkward leaving so suddenly?"

"It would have been more awkward staying."

"Oh, dear! Those Frenchmen!"

"In the singular. And I haven't even Aurora's beauty."

"But you're very nice, dear. Fresh and young."

"A skinny pigeon," said Lydia. "That, more or less, was what he called me. I'm going up to see Aurora now, and if she's asleep I'll wake her up."

Aurora was not asleep. She was sitting at her dressing-table.

She seemed to have been doing her nails, but as Lydia called softly, "Hi!" she made a quick furtive movement of her hand across her eyes before she turned.

It was almost as if she had been crying.

But her eyes were brilliant and dry as she sprang up and came towards Lydia. She was very slender, almost attenuated. Her dark dress clung round a ridiculously small waist. Her cheekbones were prominent, her lips full and pouting. She wore too much eye shadow and her eyebrows took soaring lines. She was absurdly unlike a daughter of Millicent's. Her elegance had a strangely un-English look. She was, Lydia realised, with a shock of disappointment, a stranger.

Her eager welcome died. She found herself holding out her hand formally and tilting her cheek forward for Aurora's kiss.

"Well, Lydia! You've grown up."

Lydia shrugged. "Did you think time would stop down here?"

Aurora gave a brief laugh. "Somehow I've always thought of you as a school-girl. Silly of me. You've changed enormously."

"Have I?" said Lydia absently, thinking that this was the face Philip had seen in the restaurant and immediately wanted to paint, this thin elegance, with the high cheekbones and curiously forlorn eyes. No wonder it had remained engraved on his memory.

"It's nice of you to come home for my wedding."

"It's nice of *you* to come," Lydia said pointedly.

"Oh, that. I guess I've been waiting for an excuse to make up that quarrel with the parents. Incidentally, they haven't changed. I hope Millicent isn't going to fuss like this for three solid weeks."

"She will," Lydia promised.

"Oh, lord!" A spasm of irritation crossed Aurora's face. "I wonder if I can stand it. It's this business of waiting for a licence. Would you like a drink?"

"Now?"

"It's all right. I've got a bottle of gin here. I can't bear this cocktails-at-six rule. Can you drink it with water? Or neat?"

26

Lydia grimaced. "Both I detest. But I'll force down a watery one." She added, with sudden shyness, "It *is* nice to have you home again, Aurora."

Aurora was pouring gin into a glass. She had her head bent. "I suppose I should say it's nice to be here, but frankly I feel like a fish out of water. I hadn't visualised all the fuss and excitement Millicent would generate, all this being a young and virginal bride sort of thing. After all, I'm not that young, I'm twenty-five, and as for the virginal part. . . ."

Lydia waited, but Aurora, handing her a drink, had veered from the subject and said irritably, "Mummy's so ridiculously old-fashioned. I should have remembered. But Philip seemed vaguely surprised about my lack of family, and—oh, one thing and another——"

It was the first time Philip's name had been mentioned. Lydia sipped her drink, winced at the taste, and said, "I came down in the train with Philip. So I've met him."

Aurora's eyes surveyed her over her glass. "Did you? And you spent the whole journey wondering why I was going to marry him. Or why he wanted to marry me."

"He told me how he met you. He was enraptured from that first moment."

"Enraptured? Is that the word you'd use. Yes, I suppose it is."

One could see that Aurora had become an adept at making the indirect answer, of edging the subject into a less awkward channel. "He's very impulsive," she murmured. "He's probably already regretted that day."

"Why on earth should he?" Lydia demanded. But she was remembering Philip's tall, supple form leaning over the hotel bar, his hand reaching for a glass. He was drinking double whiskies, Aurora neat gin. Was all this especially significant, or just an indication of the way they usually lived?

When Aurora made no answer to her question, she went on, "Is Philip really an explorer?"

"Why not? He says so."

"He seems to me more like a dilettante. His conversation, his luxurious tastes."

"He's a little bit of everything, botanist, anthropologist, and he's a sort of modern Gauguin—he's done some luscious paintings. He says I'm the first girl he's met since he's come back to England, so you see he's tumbled straight into my arms."

Lydia met Aurora's mocking eyes in some bewilderment. Was she very shy about showing her real feelings—or was she not in love?

"And you were ready—to tumble into his?" she murmured.

Aurora was laughing with amusement.

"Lydia, darling, how you've grown up! You're talking like a woman of the world. Millicent said you were in Paris. What happened to you there?"

Lydia shrugged. "The usual. Middle-aged wolf."

"You look as if you were able to cope."

"I ran away."

Aurora's eyes dropped. "Well, that's one way of coping. I'm all for it. Another drink?"

"No, *thank* you."

"I shall. I need it. I believe I'm going to be the jittery bride, just as Millicent hopes."

Lydia sat on the edge of the bed and said slowly, "By the way, I called at your flat this afternoon. I thought you might still be there and we could travel down together."

Aurora's head shot up. She was looking at Lydia with a strangely wary look.

"When?"

"Oh, apparently I'd missed you by about half an hour. Your neighbour, June Birch, told me."

"Oh, yes, June. She's rather a busybody, but she means well."

Lydia finished her drink, and as the anticipated warmth swam round her head she said levelly, "Who do you give the keys of your flat to, Aurora?"

Aurora didn't flush. Her face seemed to go thinner and paler.

She said, "June has one. Philip has one. At least, I think I gave him one. Why should I tell you, anyway? If it comes to that, why are you asking?"

"Because I found the door unlocked. I looked round and

28

there didn't seem to be anyone there, so I went down to ask the nearest neighbour if you were about. That was June Birch, and she said you had gone. She said you must have forgotten to lock your door and she would do so with the key you'd given her." Lydia put her glass down and looked up into Aurora's intent face. "But when we went up again the door was already locked. So there must have been someone there who slipped out as soon as I went downstairs."

"Gracious!" said Aurora. "How odd of Philip to behave like that!"

"Philip!"

"It must have been him. He was going to pick me up if he could get to London in time and we were travelling down together. But he didn't make it, so I came on alone."

"It wasn't Philip. Actually, he was ringing up just as June and I went up to your flat again."

Aurora was leaning forward. Her eyes seemed suddenly enormous, the pupils dilated and black. "Did he say where he was ringing from?"

"Yes. Piccadilly."

"I think he was having you on, Lydia. He must have just slipped round the corner."

"Why on earth would he do a thing like that?"

"Goodness knows. Probably remembered he was back in England where it isn't always the thing to be found in a lady's flat."

"But one's fiancé!"

Aurora shrugged. "He wouldn't know who you were, would he? Why should you believe him, a stranger? Simple enough, isn't it? Anyway, I'll ask him when I see him."

"You're sure it would be Philip?" Lydia persisted.

"Darling, I don't give away keys indiscriminately. Would you like to see my trousseau? What there is of it? My wedding dress is here, too. And veil. I'm not crazy about all this fuss, but I knew Millicent would be wildly disappointed if I didn't do the conventional thing. By the way, you're being my bridesmaid, of course. We'll slip up to London and get a dress for you next week. Look, this is mine."

Aurora had plunged into the wardrobe and brought out a simple, cream-coloured, satin dress which she draped over a chair. Then she was spreading out the veil, and delving into suitcases for various other items of clothing. All at once she was full of business and vivacity. Almost as if she were throwing up a smoke screen of activity to avoid another subject.

The subject of who else might still possess a key to her flat. . . .

"This is my going-away suit, though we haven't yet even decided where we're going. Probably Bournemouth! Philip says since he's only been in England six weeks nothing will drag him abroad until the end of the summer, at least. He says it's me and not a country or a fashionable holiday resort he's marrying. Look, do you like this nightdress? *Chi chi,* isn't it? And this negligée."

Scooping up the filmy garments from the suitcase something clattered to the floor. Aurora swooped to pick it up as if to conceal it. Lydia caught the glint of a gold chain.

"What's that?" she asked curiously. "A present from Philip?"

Aurora opened her hand slowly, then thrust out what it held with a sudden, almost aggressive, gesture.

"Not Philip's. My late—I should say my ex-employer gave it to me for a wedding present."

It was a heavy gold chain with an antique pendant of curiously and beautifully wrought gold set with precious stones.

"But, Aurora, that's lovely!"

"Well—not to everyone's taste. It's a bit heavy." She hung it against her slender throat.

"But it must be terribly valuable."

"I don't know. Probably not as much as you'd think. Anyway, he could afford it."

"It looks like an heirloom. Is he very wealthy?"

"I imagine so. I don't really know."

"Who is he?" Lydia persisted. "You remember, we don't know a thing that you've been doing since you left home."

"Nothing particularly exciting. Nothing secret or mysterious. I was a model until I couldn't stand it any longer, and then I

30

got this job with Armand. He's a family solicitor, you know, the old-fashioned type. Lots of elderly respectable clients. He didn't make an enormous income—who does?—but he had several wealthy aunts. The job was interesting enough. He was sorry I was leaving. I'd been his personal secretary and we'd got along pretty well." She dangled the heavy ornament over her wrist. "I expect this belonged to one of his aunts. I'm not sure yet whether I'll keep it or sell it."

"I think it's beautiful."

Aurora smiled faintly. "Do you? How sweet you are!"

"Doesn't Philip?"

"I don't know. I haven't shown it to him."

For some reason Lydia was prompted to say, "Whoever was in your flat was playing jigsaw puzzles with a piece of newspaper. Was it anything particularly significant that you had torn up?"

Aurora's eyes were suddenly quite still. They were remembering. They were, Lydia thought, re-reading what significant thing it was that had been printed on that torn sheet of paper.

"Are you—sure?"

"Perfectly sure. Because when I came back with June the paper had disappeared. I couldn't have imagined a goofy thing like that, could I?"

"No. I suppose you couldn't." Aurora spoke very slowly. "I suppose it was that bit about—I'd had some trouble about a driving licence. I'd had to go to court. Absurd, wasn't it?"

"Aurora! There was no one hurt!"

"No, I'd only scraped this wretched taxi's mudguard. But you know how it is when anyone reasonably young and good-looking goes to court. Though I must say—snooping!" She was thinking secretly again, her face closed. She picked up the gin bottle and pouring another drink swallowed it quickly, and with a disturbingly accustomed air. "Look, Lydia dear, don't mention that. You know how up in the air Millicent and Geoffrey would get. I'll have it out with Philip. Now what haven't I shown you? Oh, this cocktail dress. I'm one of those women who can't stand the little black dress. I love colours. Don't you think this is rather ravishing?"

31

"Whose car were you driving?" Lydia asked.

"Whose *car*! Oh, you mean that bother. Armand's, of course. I was going to Waterloo to meet one of his aunts. Thank heaven she wasn't in the car when I had the contretemps with the taxi. We kept it from her."

"Who is we?"

"Why, Armand—Lydia, are you *cross-examining* me?"

"I just wondered what Armand was like," said Lydia blithely.

"Oh, he's got all those doting aunts who've completely ruined him. Honestly, I was glad to leave the office."

Now she was no longer talking slowly and carefully, almost cautiously. She was chattering on in the way one would have expected her to, as an excited bride. But it was too late to deceive Lydia.

She was pretty certain the story about the car accident and the lack of a driving licence was a complete fabrication. It had been some other fact that Aurora had been destroying in that sheet of newspaper. Probably, Lydia guessed, something much more personal. A divorce case, perhaps, involving herself, or some piece of scandal she preferred Philip not to know.

But in that case she should have been more careful about handing out keys to her flat and leaving incriminating evidence lying about. Evidence which had brought a pinched look of fear to her face. . . .

It was at this stage that Aurora suddenly decided she ought to ring Philip. She dashed downstairs to do so, and Lydia, fighting an ashamed desire to eavesdrop (was Aurora going to ask Philip if he had been the mysterious intruder in her flat, and, if so, what he had discovered in the resurrected newspaper?), went slowly to her own room and firmly shut the door.

From her window, looking across the village green, she could see the red-tiled roof of the Wheatsheaf, the spire of the church, and the pond where the swans, like ballet dancers, silently drifted. It was a golden, sleepy, fairy-tale afternoon. But something, the gin probably, had made Lydia depressed and uneasy.

She couldn't think of weddings and virginal blushing brides, as Millicent was probably doing. If it came to that, neither

Millicent nor Geoffrey deserved a daughter like Aurora, who hid from them for months at a time, who had a guilty conscience about some newspaper report, who drank neat gin secretly in her room to give herself some necessary courage, and who was planning to marry a man whom she didn't love.

Now how had she come to think that last thing? Lydia was startled by her sudden unjustified intuition. Of course Aurora must love Philip. She was not, after all, the kind of girl who had to desperately seize the first available offer.

Unless whatever had been in that newspaper had made it advisable to do so. . . .

But surely Philip was not the sort of man one could do that to. Except that he seemed extremely vulnerable to feminine beauty, and may, in a rash moment, have committed himself.

And Aurora was beautiful. She was the authentic fairy-tale princess, raven dark hair, huge, brilliant eyes, features and bones of extreme fineness. Millicent must have had an intuition that she would be a beauty when she had given her that romantic name.

Had she thought, too, about possible pricked fingers that would lead to doom?

Doom! What a word to think of! How even more absurd to think that Aurora, like the fairy-tale princess, had just woken from a long sleep and still had a nightmare lingering in her eyes. Or feared a nightmare about to begin. . . .

"Lydia!" called Millicent.

Lydia went to the door.

"Yes, Millicent."

"Your father has just come in from the garden. Come down and see him. And we've decided to dress for dinner. It will be nice, with Philip coming. Aurora has gone over to the Wheatsheaf. What are you doing in your room, darling?"

"Recovering from an alcoholic nightmare," Lydia wanted to say.

For now, all at once, everything was normal again. Her head had stopped spinning. Aurora's cream satin dress was spread on the chair in her room and the wedding would be like any other wedding, except that the bride and groom would be particularly memorable; such a perfect foil for one another, she so dark and fragile, he so tall and fair.

Millicent would have photographers from fashionable papers down. Everything would be too, too conventional.

And Lydia would never know what Aurora's private nightmare had been, if indeed she had ever had one.

5

Lydia welcomed her father affectionately. He was a silent, reserved man, difficult to know, possessed of rigid principles —with which Aurora clashed violently—but both fair and kind. Life with Millicent, garrulous and gregarious, had done much to make him unbend, but it was obvious that he was not altogether happy about this sudden invasion of Aurora and her intended husband. He wanted to be reassured.

"What do you think of it, Lydia?" he asked. "Millicent is prepared to accept it as the most natural thing in the world. Why shouldn't a girl want to come home to marry, she says? But I don't know. Of course, Aurora isn't my own daughter, and I frankly don't understand her. She seems quieter, I must say, and not so moody, but she's a much more devious person than her mother. Much more."

Lydia silently agreed with that remark. Indeed, Aurora was much more devious than ever Geoffrey realised. But unless someone sprang up in the church and declared an impediment to the marriage—the melodrama of which Millicent would adore, forgetting other issues—one could do nothing but accept the situation as normal.

There was no reason for her to feel as strangely unhappy and uneasy about it as she did.

"I shouldn't worry, Daddy," she said soothingly. "Aurora knows what she's doing. She always did. And it doesn't seem to have brought her to any harm. She's rather spectacular, isn't she?"

"Too much beauty can be a bad thing," Geoffrey said soberly. "I wish she'd tell us a little more about herself. Well, perhaps she will before the wedding. If her mother can't break her down, no one can."

Aurora arrived back from the Wheatsheaf just in time to dress for dinner. Ten minutes later the telephone rang.

"It's for you, Aurora," called Millicent.

Aurora appeared at the top of the stairs.

"Me!" Her face was flushed. She had obviously had more to drink at the Wheatsheaf. "It can't be Philip. He'll be seeing me in a few minutes." She giggled. "Isn't he getting passionate?"

She came down the stairs and shut herself into the small morning-room, not intending anyone to hear her response to Philip's passion.

But her caller was not Philip after all, because while she was still in there he arrived. Lydia took him into the drawing-room. She noticed that he looked surprisingly elegant in his dinner jacket, his long, lean figure taking on a rather impressive distinction. And there was no flush, engendered by alcohol or otherwise, in his cheeks. He looked cool and contained.

"Nervous as hell," he said unconvincingly. "Am I early or late?"

"Just about right. Will you have a drink? I'm afraid there's only sherry. Daddy has a thing about not spoiling one's palate. I could nip upstairs, though, and get you some of Aurora's gin."

"Why has she got gin upstairs?"

His voice was casual. It was probably only her too acute consciousness of him that made her think he was disapproving. She found his sudden intense blue gaze even more disturbing than her memory of it.

Damn him, why did he have to look so distinguished in evening dress!

"I suppose she's nervous, too."

"Aurora! Not of me, she isn't. I'll have sherry, thank you, Lydia. What a charming room. And you fit into it extraordinarily well."

"Thank you," said Lydia absently. "Tell me, was it you in Aurora's flat this afternoon? And if it was, why didn't you say so?"

Philip took the glass of sherry she handed him, and set it down. "Do you mind telling me what you're talking about?"

"Didn't Aurora go over to the Wheatsheaf to ask you? She said she was going to. I'd better explain. I found the door of her flat unlocked and she said you were the person—or one of the persons—who had a key."

"Say that again!" said Philip. "I haven't a key to Aurora's flat."

"Then—oh, dear, I suppose I shouldn't have mentioned it——"

"I suppose you should," Philip began.

But at that moment Millicent, followed by Geoffrey, came in, and the awkward moment was over. Or postponed. Slightly distrait, Lydia performed introductions.

"How tall you are!" exclaimed Millicent, in her unexpected but disarming way. "Aurora says you've explored everywhere. Now please tell me about crocodiles. I've always been fascinated by them."

"Let me give you a sherry," Geoffrey said. "I can recommend this one. That's if you like something dry, but not too dry."

"I have one already, thank you, sir."

"Oh, splendid. Lydia's been looking after you. Where's Aurora, Millicent?"

"She's on the telephone. She thought it was Philip calling, and just couldn't get there quickly enough. Isn't it sweet, having two young people in love in the house. Your family comes from Northumberland, Philip, Aurora tells me. I suppose it was all those biting winds that sent you off to the jungle in the first place. Now do tell me about the crocodiles. Do they really have that awfully sinister saurian look?"

"Millicent, what a heavenly word. Saurian!" Lydia said.

"Yes, isn't it! I think it was in a detective story I read it first. I once had a friend who kept an alligator in a glass tank. She got quite fond of it. It was only a little one, of course. Do you know, I don't think Aurora's even dressed yet."

"Then we'll have time for another sherry," said Geoffrey calmly. "I hope you're going to be able to stand all this female fuss over a wedding, Philip."

"I rather take to it, you know," Philip lied obligingly.

Or perhaps it was not a lie, Lydia thought. Perhaps he couldn't wait for that delicious moment when Aurora, heart-breakingly lovely in her wedding dress and veil, came to stand demurely beside him at the altar.

After all, she didn't know him at all. He might be intensely conventional and sentimental.

"You've known Aurora for some time, I expect," Geoffrey went on.

"Four weeks tomorrow, to be exact." Philip's voice was blithe. "You see, I don't waste any time."

Sometimes, Lydia thought, her father possessed utterly no humour, for now he said, with some anxiety, "Goodness me, does your impulsiveness ever lead you astray?"

"Why, I think that's terribly romantic," Millicent broke in. "Just four weeks. But of course, if I were a man, I'd only have to set eyes on Aurora for one moment and I'd be lost."

"Exactly," murmured Philip. Lydia noticed that he had avoided answering Geoffrey's question. Anyway, could there be an answer, at present? He wouldn't know, until he married Aurora, whether he regretted it. There must be so much he had still to find out about her—why, for instance, no other man had swooped her up. Or why she had resisted other men. . . .

There was no time to pursue the matter further, for just then Aurora came in. She had on a filmy, grey chiffon dress, and she moved very quickly and lightly. Her cheeks were still flushed, her eyes extraordinarily brilliant. She said, in a breath-less husky voice, "Am I late? I'm terribly sorry," and crossed over to take Philip's hand and press it momentarily between hers. If it hadn't been for the traces of tears Lydia had seen earlier in the afternoon, and the rather desperate resort to the gin bottle, she would have given a very convincing act of someone deeply in love.

It may not have been an act, of course, Lydia told herself

37

fairly. It may have been genuine. But one thing at least was certain, and that was that she had had too much to drink. She was obviously almost at the stage where she might begin to sing, or burst out with some wild indiscretion.

There was no time to wonder why she was doing this, drinking too much, and getting ready to singe herself in a flame or prick her finger disastrously, as had the princess in the fairy tale. Lydia, with some desperation herself, said, "Let's go in and eat. I'm absolutely starving," and Millicent came to her support with her ingenuous, "So am I. And Philip is much too thin. We must feed him up. Have you learnt to cook, Aurora, in that flat you had?"

"Oh, I'm an absolutely wonderful cook," Aurora said in her warm, breathy voice. "You ought to taste my *coq au vin*, and my *boeuf à la mode.*"

"Oh, dear, and we've just got lamb cutlets tonight. But I'm sure Philip will appreciate truly English food after what he must have been eating in the jungle. Tell me—you sit there, Philip, beside Aurora—is crocodile edible? Oh, I don't mean the ancient monsters, like old fallen logs, but nice young things. Or do they taste horribly of mud?"

Aurora began to giggle. She looked enchanting, with her flushed cheeks, her pale slender arms emerging from the filmy dress, her slightly mussed dark hair. At least a drink too many suited her, for it took away the taut, pinched look, the strange air of apprehension. If that was the way she usually looked when she was with Philip it was no wonder he had become infatuated. Aurora, the princess, rosy from sleep and too much nectar.

Philip, with a sideways glance at Aurora, began to talk of food he had eaten in different countries. Molly, the maid, brought in the lamb cutlets and the green peas, and the meal proceeded. It seemed to Lydia to go on for hours, for Aurora's irresponsible gaiety wore off with alarming quickness and it was impossible not to see that she merely picked at her food. Once, as Philip talked, she lifted her huge eyes and they seemed to be swimming with tears. But perhaps that was the effect of the candlelight. At any rate, she had grown quite

38

silent. When they left the table and went in to sit round the fire, she sat in a corner, a little removed from everyone, like a dark-haired ghost.

When Millicent suddenly said, "Darling! Have you gone to sleep?" she started as if something much more alarming had roused her, and said quickly, "No, but almost. I'm going to get a little fresh air, when Philip goes, and then bed."

"Nothing like hastening my departure," said Philip good-humouredly. "Come along, then. You can walk me across the village green."

"Darling, put a wrap on!" Millicent cried. "It will be chilly out. And don't be late. You look dreadfully tired."

"Ten minutes, no more. Unless Philip buys me a nightcap."

"I'm not buying you any nightcaps," said Philip firmly. "You're coming to the green, and then turning round and going straight back."

Millicent wanted to wait for Aurora to come back.

"There's so much to discuss," she declared. "We haven't even talked about who we're inviting to the wedding, and it's only three weeks away! It isn't fair not to give people time. We must start making lists." She smiled happily. "I adore making lists. So satisfying. That crocodile man is rather sweet, isn't he? Though not quite——"

"Not quite what?" Lydia said sharply.

"Now, darling, I wasn't criticising him. I was merely going to say not quite the type one would have imagined Aurora choosing."

"Why not?"

"I can't really say. It's difficult to put it into words. I feel somehow they won't understand each other. Oh, well, perhaps I'm wrong. Or perhaps they like it that way."

"They must," Geoffrey said dryly. "They've been gone more than half an hour. It would take Aurora exactly five minutes to cross the green if she were not lingering. So I suggest we go to bed."

"To bed?"

"Your daughter's twenty-five, and Philip can't be much under thirty. Hardly the age one waits up for one's children."

"Oh, dear!" Millicent sighed. "And all those lovely lists I long to get at. Come along, then, Lydia. It's time you were in bed, at least."

"Even I'm an adult," Lydia reminded her good-humouredly.

But she went upstairs and firmly drew her curtains so that she would not be tempted to look across the green. Anyway, there was a slight ground mist, and Aurora, in her filmy grey dress, would melt into it, like a wraith. Philip would look as if he walked alone.

None of her business, she told herself, but as she undressed she looked at herself in the mirror with deliberately assessing eyes. If she were a man, she thought, what would she (or he, one should say) think of that form—long slender limbs, small breasts, slight hollows at the base of the neck, a face that looked elongated and anxious, eyes (what colour?), glass-green, perhaps, hair uncompromisingly straight, but thick and smooth and not too bad when well-shampooed and well-brushed. An eager, honest, quite ordinary face, she thought dispassionately, though the slight frosting of age that overlaid the mirror gave her a curious, waiting look, as if at the given moment she would burst into life.

"You'll never float down the stairs in grey chiffon," she told the waiting face, floating in its frosty haze, "but you might try dramatic colours, flame, emerald green. After all, the world doesn't hold only pawing M'sieur Bertrands. . . ."

Nor did it hold only strange, rather intriguing men with indolent watchful eyes, back from jungles and mountains. It was full of nice stockbrokers and solicitors and advertising executives and interior decorators and poets and peasants. One of them one day would find that of all things, he madly adored glass-green eyes and a long neck with delicate hollows at the base.

Climbing into bed, Lydia switched off the light, and lay smiling vaguely in the dark as she planned her dream home, and the people who would occupy it. She had almost forgotten the mists drifting over the village green, and Aurora in her smoky grey dress.

So it was not until the morning that they realised Aurora

40

had not come home. At breakfast Millicent said benignly, "Let her sleep. After a good rest she'll be much more fit to help me with those lists. I couldn't get any sense out of her yesterday. She just said, 'Let us get married. That's all I want to do,' as if we were trying to stop her! But today will be different. I'll just tiptoe upstairs after ten o'clock to see if she's ready for some coffee, and then we can get down to business. Where are you going, Geoffrey?"

"Into the garden."

"Don't go too far. We'll probably need your help. And yours, too, Lydia. This is all too exciting for words."

But it was exciting in a completely different way when Millicent found Aurora's empty and unslept-in bed.

She gave a little shriek and then called Lydia in a hushed and conspiratorial voice, "Darling! Come here! S-sh! We must keep this from Molly. But look. Aurora hasn't come home."

Lydia stood at the door of Aurora's bedroom and looked at the bed, aggressively orderly amongst the disorderliness of open suitcases and strewn belongings. The wedding dress still lay over the chair, and the other things Aurora had been showing Lydia yesterday were spread about, the filmy negligée, the new shoes, the pile of underclothing, pristine fresh and dainty, the flame-coloured cocktail dress.

The room was full of Aurora's dark, restless presence, but she was not there. The nightdress Molly had spread out for her remained untouched, the pillow smooth.

For a moment Lydia could say nothing. She had a clear memory of Philip fussing about hot water and a comfortable bed in his room at the Wheatsheaf, and although she had not seen the room they had given him she could now see, very clearly indeed, Aurora's dark hair spread on the pillow and her long pale arms lying outside the sheets.

But surely—in a small village—with their wedding so imminent—she thought incoherently. . . . Of course, they may not have stayed at the Wheatsheaf, they may have had enough sense to go farther away. Except that Aurora had no luggage and Philip no car, and it had been too late last night to catch a bus.

"What do you think?" breathed Millicent, her eyes aghast.

"We can't ring Philip up. That's one thing we can't do."

"No, of course not. I understand. Most awkward. But really! He did say he wasn't even going to buy her a night-cap, didn't he? And I wanted to wait up, but your father wouldn't let me."

"What would you have done? Gone and dragged her out of his bed?"

"Lydia, darling! Oh, dear, this is all so premature! What are we to do?"

"Wait for them to turn up, if they have the face to. Aurora will want to collect her trousseau, anyway."

Millicent pressed her hands to her cheeks. "That beautiful virginal wedding dress! Lydia, darling, how many other things don't we know about Aurora?"

"I don't know," said Lydia slowly. "I don't know."

June Birch had intimated that she had had men friends, that it would not be strange for one of them to have a key to her flat. But Philip was to be her husband in so short a time. Surely, he at least would have behaved with discretion!

"We'll have to behave as if nothing has happened," Millicent said firmly, "And Lydia dear, I think not even to tell your father. He's always been a little stern with Aurora, and I do so want her to have a beautiful wedding. Shall we just say nothing until they come. After all, they might have a perfectly good explanation."

This, however, was not so. For Philip arrived alone. He wandered in about eleven, gave Lydia his sudden smile, and said, "Where's Aurora? Isn't she up yet?"

Lydia gasped. "Don't tell me——"

"Don't tell you what?"

"That Aurora isn't with you."

"Why on earth should she be with me? Whether I like it or not, I have an austere single room at the Wheatsheaf."

"But, Philip!" Lydia looked round swiftly. Geoffrey was still in the garden and Millicent, to work off her agitation, clattering dishes in the kitchen. "She isn't home! We don't think she's been home all night. We thought she was with you."

"What?"

"What else could we think? Her bed hasn't been slept in. Her things are scattered about her room just as she left them last night. Nothing's been taken, as far as I can see."

Philip gripped Lydia's arm. "But this is nonsense. She walked across the green with me as far as the pond, and then I made her go back. I watched her until I couldn't see her for mist. Her dress melted into it. But she'd only have another hundred yards to go then. You mean she hasn't come home at all!"

"She isn't here. I told you."

"I say—what is all this? She couldn't have been kidnapped in that last hundred yards. Anyway, she would have screamed. And there'd have to have been a car which we'd all have heard."

"Yes."

"Don't just say yes like that. Say what you think."

He looked at her accusingly, his eyes brilliant and direct. It was clear that he expected her to have more knowledge of Aurora's expected behaviour than he had himself.

"What can I think?" she said helplessly. "If she really hasn't been with you she's gone somewhere else, hasn't she? I should think of her own free will."

"Of her own free will? What makes you say that, Lydia?"

"You must know yourself she isn't a person one can give orders to. I don't think I've ever known her to do something she didn't want to. So she isn't likely to have gone somewhere against her will."

"Unless she was overpowered."

"Between here and the village pond! And why? She hadn't even a handbag."

"She had other assets," Philip observed dryly. "Well, what are we to do? Sit and wait for her to turn up? Or ring the village constable?"

Millicent came in then and collapsed trembling into a chair when she heard the news. Geoffrey had to be called, and the story told again.

He said angrily, "Another prank of that girl's! I told you

43

years ago, Millicent, that she'd bring you nothing but trouble. Now look at this, all of us a laughing stock. Particularly Philip. You'd better be thankful, my boy, that this has happened before and not after your wedding."

"But, Geoffrey, darling! She might have been kidnapped. Philip says so."

"Has to save his face, hasn't he? Not very amusing being jilted on the eve of one's wedding."

Lydia glanced nervously at Philip to see how Geoffrey's cruel words affected him. Was he in anguish? His lean face had a closed look, his eyelids drooped. He was not going to parade his feelings.

He said in a contained voice, "I think we ought to look at this from every angle. You might be quite right, sir, in suggesting Aurora has changed her mind, but actually if that were so I think she would have told me. She wasn't walking in fear of me, or anything like that. Actually, it wouldn't have surprised me if she had thought twice about marrying me. She hasn't known me for long, after all. But let's look at the practical side of it. She was dressed in a thin dress and thin shoes, and some sort of wool stole. Nothing more. Not even a handbag. A girl dressed like that isn't going to catch a train or take a bus. Unless she's desperate, of course. And I didn't notice any extreme signs of desperation. Did anyone else?"

Lydia remembered the way Aurora had swallowed those gins, hastily, as if she were drowning some pain. She would have to tell Philip that later—if Aurora didn't return. But surely at any moment she would walk in, her head held arrogantly high.

"She had that long telephone conversation before dinner last night," Millicent remembered suddenly. "She shut herself in the morning room. Now I come to think of it, she never told us who she was talking to."

"She didn't have to do that," Geoffrey said fairly. "But you answered the telephone, didn't you? Who asked for her? A man or a woman?"

"A man. I thought it was Philip."

44

"And when she came down to dinner she looked awfully excited," Lydia said. "Didn't anyone else notice?"

"Well, of course she would, Lydia dear. A girl is in a constant state of excitement before her wedding."

"This may not have been because of her wedding," Lydia murmured, and then could not bring herself to look at Philip to see whether or not he winced.

"She's made a rendezvous with this fellow," Geoffrey said. "That's what she's done. She left Philip last night to go and meet him. Don't you agree, Philip?"

"Could be," Philip answered, and still his calm voice did not betray his feelings. "Perhaps she had some unfinished business to settle."

"Oh, Philip darling!" Millicent cried. "I must say that's a most charitable way of putting it. But if that is so," she looked wildly round the room, "why didn't she come back hours ago? Before midnight, in fact?"

Philip straightened his long body decisively.

"I suggest the first thing we do is put a call through to her flat. I'll do that now, if I may."

But presently he came back to say that he could get no answer. If by any chance Aurora were there she was not answering her telephone. But it didn't seem particularly likely that she was there.

"I know," Lydia exclaimed. "I'll ring June Birch. Aurora's nosy neighbour. If she's been there, or anyone else has, June will know. She has eyes made for looking through keyholes."

So there was another wait while that call was put through, and presently June's strident voice shattered Lydia's ear. "Hullo! Hullo! Who is that?"

"You won't remember me, June, but I'm Lydia Deering. Aurora's sister."

"Of course I remember you! You were here yesterday. What's up? How are the wedding bells?"

"June——" Now it wasn't so easy, because one didn't really want to admit to this busybody that Aurora was missing—"has Aurora called at her flat this morning? Early this morning or late last night?"

"Not that I know of. And I usually hear everyone who goes to her door. What are you getting at, duck? Has she run away?"

Lydia winced at the rich relish in the strident voice.

"Of course she hasn't. But she said she'd forgotten some things and would be calling at the flat some time."

"If I hear her I'll give her a message, if that's what you want." June's voice was puzzled and full of curiosity. "But she hasn't been here. There's only been one caller and that's that daft old woman. And she hasn't got a key, I know that!"

"Meaning?"

"Well, between you and me, one or two others had, as I think you gathered yesterday. What do you want me to tell her?"

"Aurora? Oh, just that—that the vicar's coming to dinner, so not to be late. It's about the wedding date, and the church decorations and so on. We were afraid Aurora might stay late in town." (And June Birch isn't believing a word of this mild village social life, and her eyes are popping out with curiosity.)

"Of course, duck. Ring me any time. I'll be here."

And she would, Lydia reflected, putting down the receiver. She would stay there with one ear waiting for the telephone and the other for suspicious footsteps going up to Aurora's flat. There wouldn't be a thing she would miss.

"No luck," she said, going back into the drawing-room. "Now that rather horrid June Birch is going to talk madly."

"Everyone's going to talk!" Millicent lamented.

"I had to make up some story about the vicar coming to dinner. June didn't believe a word of it. But she swore no one had been to Aurora's flat except someone she called that daft old woman. I haven't a clue who that would be."

"But we don't know who any of Aurora's friends are," Geoffrey pointed out. "That's going to make the whole thing extremely difficult if we have to employ a detective."

"A detective," gasped Millicent.

"I'm afraid so, dear. With Philip's approval, I think we'd better get in touch with the police station. Not that I'm suggesting anything desperate has happened, but girls frequently have been picked up by strangers in cars, and 'coshed' I think

46

is the word. Because of that possibility I don't think we should let too much time go by. What do you say, Philip?"

"I agree, sir. Especially considering the way Aurora was dressed."

It was then that Lydia got her first distinct feeling of fear. She stood at the open doors of the drawing-room and looked across the garden to the village green, innocent in the late morning sunlight. In the distance was the grey tower of the church, the tilted gravestones in the churchyard, the pond, a faint green shine where the swans floated.

Nothing could be more peaceful. But last night a ground mist had been drifting across the green: the houses, the church and the tilted gravestones had been lost in the swirling vapour. Just as Aurora, in her grey dress, had been lost. As if in a fairy story she had been turned into a swan, or spirited away to be the sleeping princess, undiscovered for years. . . .

"Lydia, what are *you* thinking?"

Philip had come to stand beside her. His voice was low and quiet, but it held a note of intense anxiety. "It wasn't me in Aurora's flat yesterday, you know. Who was it?"

"I don't know. I haven't the slightest idea."

"And this man she worked for. Armand whoever he was. Can he tell us anything?"

"I don't know. Except—oh, yes, wait a minute. I'll be back."

She was back very shortly with the heavy gold pendant in her hand.

"This is what Aurora told me Armand gave her for a wedding present. She hasn't taken it either. And I should think it's quite valuable."

Philip turned the glinting thing over in his hand. His face was puckered up in the sunlight. He looked pale and tired. "Aurora didn't strike me as the kind of girl who would forget something valuable."

"No. It means, of course, that she's coming back," Lydia said breathlessly.

"Or else that she's been given no choice but to forget it." Philip dropped the ornament back into Lydia's hand. She winced a little, suddenly not liking the feel of it, wondering where it had come from. "What are you really thinking, Lydia?"

"I don't know. But why should one's employer give one this sort of present? One might expect a week's salary, or something for the house, but not something so personal. . . ." Her voice died away. She saw the thin, hard bleakness of his face.

"But Aurora isn't like that, really," she added swiftly.

"How do you know? You haven't seen her for a long time."

"No. I suppose I don't know."

"And neither do I. I fell in love with the way she looked."

Lydia touched his hand. "It will be all right, Philip. I know it will."

"Bless you, Lydia. Of course it will."

6

The sergeant at the nearest police station was extremely regretful, but he feared they would find the lady had merely changed her mind.

"Women are liable to do that," he said with vast sadness. "Begging your pardon, Miss," he added, with scrupulous politeness, to Lydia.

He admitted that at midnight, in an evening dress, and out in the foggy dew, was a strange time to change one's mind. But that was another symptom of women's complete unpredictability and unreliability. However, he would make some enquiries at bus stations and railway stations, and find out if a woman corresponding to Aurora's description had been seen. She would have been conspicuous enough. In his opinion the telephone call had been the clue. The young lady had obviously made an assignment. Not very fair play towards one's prospective bridegroom, but there you were.

"Don't take our philosophic friend personally," Philip said to Lydia as they left the police station.

Lydia shrugged.

48

"How do you know I wouldn't be like that, too?" (Wandering about lonely roads at night in a chiffon dress, and high-heeled shoes . . . Lying dead in a ditch. . . .) Suddenly she shivered.

"Philip, you must know! Would Aurora have done this to you?"

"Why must I know?" His voice was flat, giving nothing away.

"Surely you knew whether she loved you or not."

"I hope she loved me."

"But you weren't sure?"

His disconcertingly bright eyes were turned on Lydia.

"No. Frankly I wasn't. I felt I could very well have got her on the rebound."

"That she was fretting for someone else?"

"She was distrait at times, yes."

"This man who telephoned last night?"

"But we don't know who that was, do we?"

"This hypothetical character, then. If you must know, Aurora was drinking too much yesterday."

Philip grimaced. "Reminds me I'm thirsty myself. Let's have a drink somewhere."

"But shouldn't we go home? If Aurora has arrived——"

"If Aurora has arrived back from her stroll last night she can wait a little while for us. Can't she?"

"Oh, poor Philip!" Lydia exclaimed involuntarily, and then, because his look of angry cynicism was for someone else, and because she cried too easily anyway, tears suddenly filled her eyes and ran over on to her cheeks.

"It looks more like poor Lydia," he said. "I should be shedding tears, not you."

"It's only that—supposing something has happened to her. We shouldn't only guess that she's run off with another man. I thought she seemed frightened, or upset anyway, when I told her about someone being in her flat."

"Nothing's happened to her," Philip said curtly. "She knows how to take care of herself. You'll see. Come along and have this drink."

But at the bar in the Wheatsheaf Lydia had the greatest

trouble in controlling more tears. If Philip, to Aurora, had been a substitute for someone else, so was she now to Philip. And it was no fun at all. Because she realised with dismay what was happening to her, had indeed been happening since the moment of meeting on Waterloo station yesterday. She was falling in love. And nothing could be less propitious than to fall in love with a man whose mind held only Aurora's lovely face.

Into the disrupted house, with Millicent alternately hysterical and in a state of collapse, Geoffrey filled with his silent anger, and Aurora's room inhabited mutely by her discarded trousseau, Aurora's letter came as an anti-climax.

It arrived the next morning after the phlegmatic sergeant had telephoned to report that he had found no trace of any young woman in evening dress, nor had any unidentified victim of assault been picked up. It justified all he had predicted and all that Philip had bitterly guessed.

The letter was addressed to Lydia and postmarked London.

"Lydia darling,

"I'm too ashamed to write to Philip or to Millicent. I am a complete heel. But Philip knows I was never really in love with him. There was someone else, and I thought it wouldn't work, but it is going to, after all. He came for me last night and I just went, like that, because I hadn't the courage to come back and tell you. I don't expect Millicent and Geoffrey to forgive me, but I hope Philip will. And if ever this happens to you, Lydia dear, as it is all too likely to happen to any girl, you will understand.

"Be a darling, please, and send me that gold pendant. It's the only thing I want because I couldn't use the clothes intended for my marriage to Philip. Send it care of the G.P.O., Edinburgh.

"And don't criticise me. Wish me luck instead.
"Blessings, Aurora."

There was a remorseful postscript.

"I do know I'm a heel, but make everyone understand."

Was one to show this curiously callous letter to Philip? What else was there to do, since Aurora hadn't had the decency to write to him herself?

The writing was scrawled and shaky, as if she had had more than one neat gin before taking up her pen. There was a blot in one place that could almost have been a spilt tear, if one didn't get the undertone of suppressed malice and triumph all through the letter.

Lydia had an impulse to tear it angrily into bits and show it to nobody.

But her impulse instead brought back another memory— that of the torn newspaper in Aurora's flat.

Of course, it must have contained some information about Aurora's mysterious lover, or perhaps about both of them. It would have been this lover, retrieving the paper in Aurora's flat that day, curious to see what she had kept or destroyed. Which made one think that the evidence in it could be incriminating.

Now one had to get it and see for oneself. It was fortunate that she had noted the date.

If Aurora's family could not be told whom she was marrying, it was fair that they should find out by other means.

Because of her anger over Aurora's behaviour Lydia forgot to feel relieved that Aurora had not been found dead in a ditch. The letter still in her hand—the postman had come before Millicent, exhausted after a sleepless night, had come down—Lydia impulsively sat down to write a reply.

"Dear Aurora,

"If you want your pendant you must come and get it. Write and arrange a place for us to meet, but I will not be your go-between by post. I feel very ashamed of you, and will only understand, as you have asked me to, when you have justified your behaviour. If, indeed, you can.

"Lydia."

She was not accustomed to being vindictive. She shed tears, afterwards. But that was when she went through the ordeal of breaking the news to Millicent and Geoffrey.

After that she walked across to the Wheatsheaf to see Philip, posting her letter on the way.

"Millicent says thank goodness Aurora isn't murdered, and Geoffrey says she deserves to be," she told Philip bluntly. "What do you say?"

Philip had read the letter. He put his hand over Lydia's.

"You don't have to apologise for your sister. Is this her handwriting, by the way?"

"I think so," said Lydia, startled. "But don't you know it?"

"No. We communicated by telephone. Seems I didn't know anything about Aurora except her face." His voice was wry.

"But if it weren't her handwriting, whose would it be?"

"Whose indeed? And why?"

"Philip, I'm afraid you'll have to believe it," Lydia said gently.

His eyes flew open to give her one of his long, thoughtful stares.

"That wasn't wishful thinking for my own benefit. Believe it or not, it's Aurora's health I was thinking of. One wonders who matters most, this secret lover or the pendant. Lydia, this is where we go to London. I've exhausted the possibilities of the Wheatsheaf, anyway. And I've an exhibition of paintings to organise. One's life doesn't stop—or so the books tell one."

This wry emotion was all he was going to show. Lydia said impulsively, "All girls don't behave like that, Philip."

"Strangely enough, I don't think even Aurora behaves like that. Let's go back to London and look up this old newspaper you talked about, and call on June Birch. We might have dinner somewhere later. Bring some luggage with you. Don't travel light as Aurora did."

"Philip, what are you getting at?"

At last his long intelligent face lost its cynical look, and became purely perplexed.

"I don't really know. I just can't quite believe this is true. It's too slick, somehow. And there's that mercenary element of the pendant which, knowing Aurora even a little, doesn't seem in character. I take it you're not sending it to Edinburgh?"

"No."

"Good girl. Bring it with you. It's time, anyway, that we made the acquaintance of Aurora's ex-employer. The mysterious Armand. And his aunts."

The page from *The Daily Reporter* of the third of April told them exactly nothing. They had called at the newspaper offices on their way from Waterloo, and anticipating finding the answer to a puzzle had eagerly studied that issue. But there was nothing in it remotely relating to Aurora Hawkins, unless she were using another name. Even then there was no event which could correspond with any of her possible behaviour.

Lydia sighed over a long argument in the House of Commons, and Philip dismissed an attempted murder in Glasgow, a divorce case in which none of the participants was under the age of forty, and a brief paragraph about the unidentified body of an elderly woman discovered at the foot of a cliff.

"That torn newspaper can't have meant anything," Lydia said disappointedly.

"Unless they'd got hold of the wrong page."

"But there's nothing in any of this paper that could be associated with Aurora. Certainly nothing about a motor accident, but I never believed what she said about that."

"Why would she be lying?"

"Because she didn't want to tell me what really was in the paper, I suppose."

"We've just discovered there's nothing," Philip pointed out.

"So we have. Not even anything about this Armand she worked for. Did you read all the marriage notices?"

"I did. Supposing she had used a false name she could have been May Smith or Joan Brown or Hepzibah what's-her-name."

Lydia tucked her hand in his arm. "Don't let it hurt you."

He gave his faint ironic smile. "Let's skip the obvious, shall we? We're getting nowhere here, so what shall we do? Come to my rooms and I'll paint you."

She moved away from him, turning the newspaper neatly in its file. "I'd have thought you'd have learnt your lesson about picking up stray women to paint."

He could not be deceived. She knew by his sidelong look that he was aware of the unspoken words beneath her rebuke.

"You're eminently paintable," he said, in answer to her private grief. "I can see you against a dark red curtain. Simple, dramatic."

The clerk behind the desk was watching them, listening inquisitively.

Lydia tilted her chin. "Then come on, Annigoni. We're wasting our time."

"Gauguin, the critics say. We must listen to the critics. But you haven't seen my dusky belles. You must come to my studio. All right, I won't press you just at the moment."

They had to keep their conversation on this light plane, otherwise they would both see Aurora sitting, poised and beautiful, in Philip's studio, waiting.

And Lydia, to her shame, knew that she couldn't bear Aurora to be there. Even though it was essential to discover her whereabouts.

"Are you coming to Aurora's flat with me?" she asked.

"You're going there?"

"Of course. To see if anything has happened since yesterday. I found the key among the things Aurora left at home. We can talk to June Birch, if no one else. And besides there's something else. I've decided to stay in the flat until Aurora returns."

"Whatever for?" She had his full, slightly alarmed attention.

"Because surely it's a sensible thing to do. I'll know when Aurora comes back, and if she doesn't—I mean, if there's really anything wrong—I can perhaps find out who her friends are, who rings her up or writes her letters."

"And who has a key to her door," Philip said sharply.

"Well, that, too. But I shouldn't think that's a thing to worry about because I expect it's the man she says she's marrying. So they'll both come back. And don't fuss about it, Philip, please. It's something I'm doing because Aurora is my stepsister and it's my duty. I used to be very fond of her. I suppose I still am, though I don't know her any more. But if she is married to someone else it's no longer any of your business what happens to her. So don't make objections about what I'm going to do. Because I simply won't listen."

Philip took her arm.

"Shall we talk about this outside? And I intend to make strenuous objections. Not because of Aurora. Because of you."

They had stepped out into the sunlight. The traffic roared past. A flower-seller was holding out a bunch of yellow roses.

"You, Lydia," Philip repeated.

"I did hear you the first time." She doubted if he heard her small voice over the sound of passing cars. Of course he was thinking of her. He had lost one of the sisters. It wouldn't be sense to lose another, whether he loved her or not. "But I still mean to stay there," she added. "And why not? I have to get a job and I must live somewhere. Aurora won't mind. I'll explain when she comes back."

Philip took the bunch of roses from the flower-seller and paid for them. "Then we might as well have some flowers to brighten up the place."

Everything appeared to be exactly the same in Aurora's flat, except for the letters lying in the hall. Actually, there was only one letter. The other three envelopes were unsealed and contained circulars or bills.

The letter was addressed to Miss A. Hawkins. The writing was sprawling and shaky. It could have been written by someone aged, or, as Philip suggested, someone writing with his left hand.

"Why?" Lydia asked bluntly.

"To disguise the writing, of course. If you're looking for a mystery, we might as well think one up."

"We'll soon see," said Lydia with decision. "I'm going to open this."

The sheet of paper inside the envelope, covered with the same shaky writing, was a letter, old fashioned and formal.

"Dear Miss Hawkins,
"I apologise for writing to you again, and do beg you to forgive these incursions into your valuable time. The weather

55

has been so charming that I ventured forth to call on you yesterday. But alas, without the good fortune of finding you at home. However, the outing benefited me. I walked all the way both ways, and although this is trying on shoe leather, it did save bus fares which, as you know, are not exactly negligible. The purpose of this letter, though, is to tell you that my sister has not yet returned and I am really growing most anxious about her. I called again at her hotel, only to be told that she had not come back nor had they heard from her.

"My landlady is *not* a patient woman, and is growing very disagreeable. She says she will allow me to stay one more week, but only on condition that my sister sends my remittance as usual.

"If she has forgotten to send it and I cannot discover where she is I am in a very distressing position, as I am sure you will see, my dear Miss Hawkins. I only trouble you with this long complaining letter in the hope that your kindness will persuade Mr. Villette to arrange something for me until my sister returns. You remember that you promised to do what you could.

"Already in writing this I feel happier. As indeed I should be, with the weather so charming, and today, do you know, there were *two* letters for me. Such a surprise.

"But soon I fear I shall not be able to buy more postage stamps. And then the postman will neglect me.

"Dear Miss Hawkins, please write if you or Mr. Villette have any news of my sister.

"Your troubled friend,
"Clara Wilberforce."

"She's nuts," said Philip.

"She's in trouble," said Lydia. "Aurora must have been helping her."

"Or this Villette fellow."

"Yes. That must be Armand. The mysterious Armand."

"Of course. Clever girl. He's a solicitor. This crazy creature must be one of his clients. Some solicitors have flocks of elderly female clients."

56

"Poor Aurora! If she was being pursued even out of the office like this, no wonder she ran away."

"She ran away from me," Philip pointed out.

"Not away from you. To someone else. There's a difference."

"It's so fine it eludes me. Well, what are we to do about the crazy Miss Clara?"

"What *can* we do? She doesn't even put an address on this letter. She must be the woman June Birch said had called yesterday. I should say she's Mr. Villette's affair. Let's look up the telephone book and see if there's an Armand Villette a solicitor."

"There is!" Philip exclaimed, a few minutes later. "Armand Villette, solicitor, Pyne Street, W.C.1. That's Bloomsbury, isn't it? That must be our man. The famous Armand. Do you think Clara Wilberforce is one of his aunts?"

"Hardly. She doesn't address him as dear nephew. Yet she appeals to him for help, as if he would know about her missing sister. Oh, Philip!" Lydia pressed her fingers to her lips.

"What?"

"There *was* something in that newspaper. The only thing that could be associated with this. Don't you remember? The—" she winced at saying the words, the body of an unidentified woman."

"I don't see why we should suppose——" Philip began slowly. "No, that's a very long chance."

"But Aurora had kept the paper for some reason."

"That may have been accidental. Perhaps Miss Wilberforce had brought it to show her."

"But it wouldn't be accidental that someone else was interested in it."

Lydia met his eyes reluctantly. Apprehension was stirring in her again. What was this they were stumbling into? A runaway bride? Or something more, something worse? Something from which Aurora had to be saved?

The sudden ringing of the doorbell made them both start violently. Then they both laughed and Philip went to open the door.

It was, as might have been expected, June Birch.

"I heard voices," she said heartily. "I must say I didn't think you'd be back so soon. Are you married already and skipping the honeymoon? Sensible, I call that. Saving all those hotel bills. Oh, it's not Aurora with you!"

"No, it's me," Lydia apologised.

"The beautiful younger sister," Philip said with a flourish, and suddenly it seemed years ago to Lydia that she had used that expression on the telephone.

"Can I come in? Where's Aurora? Jilted you?"

Her inquisitive eyes searched Philip's face, and then popped visibly at his nod.

"I'm afraid so, Mrs. Birch."

"Call me June," she said loudly, to cover her embarrassment. "Well, I'll be—— But she was rather a flier, you know. I wondered if you'd find that out."

"The gentleman who had a key to her flat?" Philip suggested, with his elaborately impersonal air.

"Who was he?" Lydia asked eagerly. "We wouldn't ask if it weren't important now to know."

"Afraid I can't tell you." June tossed her pale yellow curls. "Oh, not that I wouldn't have found out if I could have, but Aurora was pretty cagey, you know."

"You mean you never saw him?"

"He came at—shall we say—discreet hours? I only saw his back once, going up the stairs. He was tall, well dressed. Wore a homburg. City type. That's all I can tell you, really."

"Young?" Lydia asked.

"Youngish. Rather like him, as a matter of fact." She indicated Philip with a nod. "Back view, anyway."

Philip laughed briefly. "Some people fall for similar types. Aurora probably did. It would have been more comfortable to know she didn't like them in the plural. Do you think, by the way, that he was the man she worked for?"

"I couldn't say. She never mentioned names. But putting two and two together, I'd say he probably was."

"Then why the devil," said Philip with contained fury, "didn't she marry him long ago?"

"That's what I wondered, too. But you never know, do you?

58

I expect he had a wife already. Do you mean to say she's run off with him now? Wife or not?"

"We don't know what she's done," Lydia said. "But there are several things we'd like to know. First, the old woman called Miss Wilberforce. You've seen her, haven't you? You said an old woman called yesterday."

"That one! Old goofy! Yes, she called all right. Aurora wouldn't fret about missing her."

"Why?"

"I can't tell you. I told you your sister was pretty cagey. But I do know she didn't always open her door to that old woman. If you ask me, she was nervous of her."

"Nervous?"

"Well, something. How do I know? It might have been the gentleman who made her act all trembly."

"Had this old woman called often?" Philip asked.

"No. Only in the last week or so. She wanted something, I think. Don't ask me what. I say, this is a do, isn't it?"

Lydia looked with acute distaste at June's eager, protuberant eyes and air of expectant relish. It was going to be difficult to endure this snooping kind of neighbour, but it must be done, even with friendliness. For June might conceivably be useful.

At least she would be someone to whom to turn if, by any chance, it was not the owner of Aurora's door key who was now in the process of marrying her.

If the smart city type with the homburg was still coming up the stairs, softly and at discreet hours.

"It isn't amusing," she said. "But actually it suits me in a queer way, because I want a flat in London for a while and I'll stay here until Aurora comes back."

"You won't be scared?"

"Scared?" said Lydia haughtily.

"What do you think?" June appealed to Philip. "With these goings on of your fiancée's—excuse me, she isn't that any longer, is she?"

"I couldn't be more opposed to Lydia staying here," Philip said flatly.

"Oh, Philip! Don't be absurd!"

June's eyes went from one to the other of them in knowing amusement.

"I'll leave you to fight it out between you. I'll be glad to be of help if you stay, duck, but I sleep like a log after midnight. So it's no use your screaming then."

When she had gone Lydia looked round the living-room, comfortable, tasteful, tidy, except for a faint film of dust on the polished furniture. She noticed things now that she hadn't done on her first brief visit. For instance, the room was furnished in a way that one would hardly have felt was within the scope of a typist who had no private allowance. The painting over the fireplace looked like an original. The lamp on the low table was surely alabaster. Lydia suddenly remembered an elaborate jewel-box on Aurora's dressing-table. And without knowing why she was thinking of the heavy gold pendant that was packed in her own bag at the moment.

That, Aurora had said quite frankly, Armand had given to her. Armand Villette, the solicitor in Bloomsbury who also was supposed to be helping the daft Miss Wilberforce. Were the other valuables in the flat from him? And in that case was it he who had run off with Aurora?

There seemed to be little doubt about it.

"I'd better unpack," she said absently.

Philip looked more closely at the picture over the fireplace, the only one in the room.

"I'm sure it is, you know. A Monet."

"No!"

"Much more valuable than that pendant she's fretting about. And yet she lets people wander about with spare keys."

"Well, if those people, or I should say that person, was the donor of the picture," Lydia said lucidly, "it would be all right, wouldn't it?"

"Of course. Logical. But the whole thing doesn't make a great deal of sense, does it. Lydia, I don't want you to stay here."

"Why ever not?"

"You're too young to be alone."

"Oh, nonsense!" She added shrewdly, "I won't be alone the way Aurora was. Anyway, there's a chain on the door. I promise to use it at nights."

"It isn't necessary for you to stay here."

"Probably not. But I want to. I want to know who rings up, or calls. I—I'm not happy about any of this, Philip."

"I'm not madly enthusiastic myself."

"I think Aurora might need our help." She looked round, trying to suppress a shiver. "I don't know why, but this place —it's so pleasant and ordinary, and yet—— Why hadn't you noticed before that that was a Monet?" she demanded.

"I had. But Aurora said it was only a copy. She'd bought it in Paris."

"And you didn't prove it?"

"No. To tell the truth, I wasn't thinking much about it at the time."

Lydia shivered again. Aurora was there, smiling her secret smile, enticingly lovely. No, she wasn't, the room was frighteningly empty. And Lydia didn't really want to stay. She longed to go to some impersonal hotel bedroom. Or perhaps to curl up happily on a hard couch in Philip's studio.

All she said was, "I didn't know Aurora had ever been to Paris. But I don't really know anything about her, as I said." She went to draw the curtains, and turned to see him watching her. "Now do stop worrying about my being here. I have a chain on the door and June Birch with her sharp ears sticking out downstairs, and the telephone. You can ring six times a day if you want to. But you don't have to. Actually, you don't really have to bother any more about any of this. Aurora has let you down, you're quite free to go back to your tropical islands if you want to. I can sort out Miss Wilberforce and the expensive presents, and what Armand is going to have to say about it all when I ring in the morning."

She raised her eyes to him. He looked very tired. His face was pale and had a far-off look. He was watching her without seeing her. He was seeing Aurora's head against that scarlet cushion on the couch. . . . Or that was how it seemed to be

61

until suddenly he caught her arm so tightly that it was an effort not to wince with pain.

"I'd kiss you, Lydia, but not in this place. You absurd child! Come and let's find somewhere to eat. There's nothing like food to bring one back to sanity."

7

Contrary to her expectations, Lydia went fairly contentedly to bed in Aurora's bed. She was very tired. The anxiety and excitement of the day had been completed by dinner in a small restaurant in Maida Vale, with Philip being attentive and charming only because presently the dreaded lonely hours would be on him. That had been the biggest strain of all, because she had longed so much to think that Philip was perfectly contented in her company, when she knew very well that it was impossible for him to be so. But his indolent gaze told nothing. And finally the dim room, the black-coated waiters, the pink-shaded lights and the white tablecloths swam in a sleepy fog.

She left Philip at the door of Aurora's flat, nodding amiably but drowsily to all his injunctions. Chain on door, telephone by bed, don't get any crazy ideas and try to carry them out without telling me, don't go out looking for this old woman, ring me immediately if you're worried.

Finally he left without kissing her.

She listened to his steps dying away down the stairs. She knew he had not particularly wanted to kiss her.

She lay in Aurora's bed wondering where Aurora was sleeping. Hazily she imagined her shut away somewhere, lying on a magnificent bed, dust and cobwebs growing round her. . . .

Then she slept herself, and woke only to hear Aurora coming very slowly up the stone stairs and fumbling at her door to get in.

When she found the door was locked—and apparently she hadn't got a key—she began to rattle at the letter-box.

After a moment of that (and by this time Lydia was fully awake and sitting up in bed, breathing suffocatingly), whoever was at the door began to move away.

Lydia listened to the slow, deliberate footsteps pacing to the head of the stairs, pausing, beginning to descend a few steps, pausing again, returning. . . .

Was this the mysterious person who had the key to Aurora's flat? If it were, he was behaving as if he were drunk, unable to find the keyhole, unable even to decide whether or not he had a key.

Chiefly because she didn't want to be found helplessly in bed in a nylon nightdress she got up and put on a housecoat. She was trembling as she tried to do up the buttons. It seemed to be bitterly cold.

She listened to the fumbling at the letter box again, and with a tremendous effort of will made herself go and switch on all the lights, so that the innocent bright interior of the flat sprang to life.

Now she was all right. She had dismissed the nightmare. She was in Aurora's flat and there was someone at the door who either had lost his way, or his key. That was all.

The time, she noticed with cool detachment, was just after midnight. The discreet time June Birch had talked about? And was June sleeping heavily now, beyond waking with a scream?

The letter-box rattled again. Lydia, clinging to her self-control, went into the hall. Then she nearly did scream. For she could see the stubby fingers, curiously foreshortened, waving through the slit of the box.

There was something pathetic, helpless, and quite sinister about them.

She could do nothing but press her own fingers to her mouth, stifling the scream that was not going to bring her any help, even from June Birch.

She had to force herself to open the door. She knew that. She braced herself, and took hold of the knob.

Then it was that the voice, speaking in a loud whisper, came through the pushed-open letter box.

"Miss Hawkins! I can see the light. I know you're there. Please open the door and let me in."

Lydia flung open the door and the elderly woman almost tumbled inside. She steadied herself and gave a small, pleased laugh.

"Oh, there you are, dear. I'm so thankful to find you home. I hope I'm not *too* late, but it was unavoidable."

It was anti-climax, after all. Lydia's legs abruptly felt very shaky, and she wanted to sit down. Also, somehow, she wanted to laugh. For her visitor was strange, a little wild-haired, pathetically shabby, unapologetic about her extraordinary behaviour, but at once curiously endearing.

"I'm not Miss Hawkins," she said. "I'm her sister. But do come in and tell me what's wrong."

The woman started back, staring at Lydia's unfamiliar face.

"Of course you're not Miss Hawkins. I can see now. How stupid of me. I didn't know she had a sister. She didn't tell me. How odd."

"Why should it be odd that she didn't tell you?"

The faded, round blue eyes, with child-like candour, looked up into her face. "Because our conversation was always about sisters, you see. Always. I've lost mine, too."

"I'm sorry!"

"Oh, she's not dead. I haven't lost her that way. She's just missing. She left her hotel without letting me know, and she hasn't come back, or written to me. And I'm really in the greatest possible distress."

Here, the old woman swayed a little, and Lydia sprang to help her into the living-room and settle her on the couch.

"You're exhausted, Miss Wilberforce. You are Miss Wilberforce, aren't you? I'm going to make you some tea."

The woman settled back among the cushions, like a plump, elderly, stray cat, thankfully finding a welcome. Her bag, a large shabby black one, bulging noticeably, she placed carefully beside her.

"How delightful tea would be. And at such an unconventional hour. I do apologise for that. But circumstances dictated. Yes, I am Clara Wilberforce. How did you know?"

"I guessed. Actually, I read your letter to Aurora because——" She hesitated, the strange coincidence of two missing sisters striking her. Had that fact any significance? "I thought I should," she added. "You said my sister had been helping you."

"With moral courage, yes. She was *so* sweet and kind. She assured me Blandina would return. But she hasn't, you know. There hasn't been a word from her. Not a word."

Lydia looked thoughtfully at the small, round, anxious face. A crab-apple face, rosy and wrinkled, ready to sparkle with humour and gaiety, but now only lugubrious and very tired. Why, she wondered suddenly, had Aurora refused sometimes to open the door to her, as June Birch had said? One could not conceivably be afraid of a little creature like this. Although, of course, if the visits were made at such an unconventional hour as this it was understandable that Aurora might have grown annoyed and impatient.

"I'll make the tea," she said. "Then we'll talk. You can tell me everything."

But when she came back to the living-room with a tray she smiled with amusement, and something approaching tenderness. For her strange guest had fallen asleep. Settled into her nest of cushions, her head tipped sideways, her shabby black coat tucked round her, her plump little hand still clutching the handle of the bulging handbag, she slept like a child.

Lydia put down the tray and went to the bedroom to get a rug. This she laid gently over the little round form. Then she replaced the chain on the door, switched out the lights, and went quietly back to bed. Now she could sleep.

She was aroused, in full daylight, by an insistent prodding on her shoulder. Miss Wilberforce beamed down at her.

"The postman, dear! Your mail. Nothing for me, I'm sad to say."

Lydia sat up, taking the letter (which looked like an advertising circular) from her.

"But how could there be anything for you, Miss Wilberforce? You don't live here."

"No, of course, I realise that. It's only that whenever I move away from home I make arrangements for my mail to be sent on. I'm seldom neglected, you know. My bag is full of letters." She patted the shabby bag, explaining its rotundity. "I'm the greatest correspondent," she said with pride.

"I hope you slept well, Miss Wilberforce."

"Very well, thank you. It was so kind of you to let me stay. Otherwise it would have been a doorway for me. It really would, you know. Or perhaps a churchyard. My landlady turned me out. We had words, to be quite truthful. I was about to explain that to you last night when I so rudely fell asleep. But now it's morning, and I can say thank you from my heart."

Lydia pondered, and got nowhere.

"Let's have coffee," she said helplessly. "Or do you prefer tea? And then you must tell me the whole story."

It was a strange story, and Lydia's heart was beating uncomfortably fast when Miss Wilberforce had finished. For shortly she had to telephone Armand Villette. And she was overcome with stupid, unreasonable apprehension.

The telephone rang, and it was Millicent to ask if Lydia had any news, and to recount, at great length, the embarrassment and anti-climax she and Geoffrey were suffering from. Making explanations to the vicar, putting Aurora's trousseau out of sight, worrying. There had been no more letters and they were still completely in the dark.

Lydia said that she and Philip were also still in the dark, but made no mention of her guest. That would be too complicated to start relating to Millicent by telephone. Anyway —it might be better that Millicent and her father remained in the dark.

With Philip it was another matter. As soon as he telephoned, sounding pleased to hear her voice, the heavy feeling of apprehension lightened. She looked to see that Miss Wilberforce was pottering usefully in the kitchen, washing dishes and tidying, and began the story.

66

"Her sister Blandina has always made her an allowance, you see. She has absolutely no other means. Blandina was apparently very wealthy and refused to let Miss Wilberforce apply for a pension. She can do that now, of course, but it will take time, and anyway, who can live and pay rent on an old-age pension?"

"Stick to the point," Philip reminded her.

"Well, the point is that one day Blandina's money didn't arrive (she always sent it in cash because that was simpler for Miss Wilberforce), and when Miss Wilberforce called at her hotel in Bayswater—she can tell us exactly where it is—they told her that her sister had left several days ago, taking her luggage and saying she didn't know when she would be back, if ever."

"With not a word to this old girl?"

"Not a word. Although she said that wasn't surprising because they had never got on. Miss Wilberforce had always muddled along, doing foolish things, and Blandina, who had married well, despised her and was ashamed of her. The allowance was merely a cash transaction because of family duty. But it was understood that Miss Wilberforce should never intrude on Blandina's social life, whatever that was."

"And so?" said Philip.

"When the allowance didn't turn up for two weeks Miss Wilberforce remembered the name of Blandina's solicitor and went there."

"Armand Villette, of course."

"That's right. But she never got to see Mr. Villette himself. She only saw Aurora. Actually, this was only last week, and apparently Mr. Villette was away or unavailable or something. Aurora had promised to talk to him about Miss Wilberforce and see what could be done. They had handled Blandina's affairs once, but not at present. Anyway, that's where things stood last week. Then Aurora went away without doing anything about her, and she still hadn't been able to see Mr. Villette, so she was getting desperate. If she hadn't found me here she was going to the police."

"Where is she now?"

"In the kitchen. The door's shut. She won't hear. She lives in a world of her own, anyway."

"Ga-ga?"

"In the nicest way. Her ghastly landlady said she had to be out of her room by eight o'clock last night, so she walked here, all the way from Battersea. She was exhausted and just fell asleep on the couch. I can't think how Aurora could have gone away without saying a word about her."

"How do you know she didn't? She probably told this Villette fellow and he hasn't bothered. Penniless old women can be quite a trouble to a solicitor, especially if he really doesn't act any longer for Blandina."

"Philip!"

"Yes?"

"Do you think that bit in the paper about the unidentified——" She had her hand cupped round her mouth to stop any possibility of Miss Wilberforce overhearing. Then she couldn't go on with what she was saying, and finished instead, "That *was* the paper that Aurora had torn up."

"H'mm."

"That's not saying yes or no. All right, I suppose neither of us can say that. But I'm going to ring Mr. Villette as soon as his office opens."

"And what are you going to say when you speak to him?"

"I'm going to ask to come and see him on a matter of importance. I'll tell him I'm Aurora's sister. He'll see me," she added confidently.

"And supposing," said Philip slowly, "he is at this moment in Edinburgh with Aurora?"

"Yes, I know, I'd thought of that. I'll insist on getting in touch with him there. His secretary will know how to. Philip, come over as soon as you can."

Miss Wilberforce professed herself enchanted with Philip. She smoothed her unruly grey hair coquettishly, and said significantly, "Ah! I mustn't play gooseberry. You two don't want an old woman around."

Lydia was crossly aware that she was blushing. Philip gave

68

his slow, maddening smile and said, "We're delighted to have you, Miss Wilberforce. We wanted to meet you."

"Did you really? How nice of you. Your Lydia is so sweet. Not a word of reproach about the time I arrived last night. I was horrified when I found it was past midnight. It had taken me much longer than I had anticipated in coming across the park. And I hadn't lurked."

"I'm going to put through this telephone call," Lydia said to Philip. "Talk to Miss Wilberforce for a few minutes."

But although the reassuring sound of friendly conversation went on in the living-room, she still found her hand shaking as she dialled the number. Why should she be so ridiculously nervous of a man she had never met?

A woman's crisp voice answered.

Lydia controlled the tremor in her own voice. "Can I speak to Mr. Villette, please?"

"Who is calling?"

"Miss Deering. He won't know who I am, but you might tell him I'm Aurora Hawkins's step-sister."

"Hold the line, please."

Philip's head stuck round the door. Lydia held up her crossed fingers. "He's there!" she whispered. He disappeared again, and the efficient voice in her ear said, "I'm sorry, Miss Deering, but Mr. Villette has a client with him at present. Can you leave a message, or can he call you back?"

Stalling? Lydia wondered. But why? At least he was not in Edinburgh with Aurora, or wherever she was. Was she relieved about that? She didn't know. She decided to make quite sure of his reactions.

"Actually, I'd like to see him if I could. I want to talk to him about my sister who I'm afraid may be in trouble, and also I have a sister of an old client of his here. Miss Clara Wilberforce. Her sister is Mrs. Blandina Paxton. Would you tell him both matters are urgent."

She waited again for what seemed an endless time. Then the voice came back. "Mr. Villette could see you this afternoon, Miss Deering. At two-thirty. Would that be convenient?"

The office was on the second floor of a tall, narrow, time-blackened house near to a Bloomsbury Square. Lydia climbed the linoleum-covered stairs, and was out of breath at the top, not because of her physical condition but because of the way her heart was beating.

Was she building too much round Armand Villette's significance in the Aurora mystery?

Had she imagined that Aurora was hiding something more than affection for him? Was he the man who had the key to Aurora's flat? And where did Clara Wilberforce come into all this? She would soon know.

The time was two-thirty, and in a few moments she would meet Armand face to face.

There was no need to be nervous because Philip was strolling about, just out of sight round the corner. He had wanted to come with her, but she had said flatly no. Armand was much more likely to be frank if she were alone. And what, she asked, could happen to her in a respectable solicitor's office in mid-afternoon?

If he were respectable, Philip had retorted, and had added that if Lydia were not down within half an hour he was coming up to announce himself.

This was reassuring and it made her happy. Not that she was anything more than merely nervous. But it was wryly comforting that Philip was acting as her protector.

There was no one in the small reception office. Lydia stood at the counter, and looked across at a desk on which stood a typewriter shrouded in its plastic cover.

The owner of the efficient secretarial voice must be still away at lunch, though it was strange that she should cover her typewriter for the space of an hour.

Someone, however, had heard her come in, for one of the inner doors opened and a man appeared.

He came across to her holding out his hand.

"Miss Deering, I believe. Aurora's sister. This is a pleasure. Do come into my office."

He was middle-aged, of medium height, rather stout, grey-haired, ruddy-cheeked. He had large, round, pale-blue eyes

70

and wore horn-rimmed spectacles. He was the facsimile of a million other business men. Quite unmemorable.

As always when she suffered from anti-climax Lydia's legs became unsteady. She walked carefully round the counter and crossed over to the door which the man held open.

"You're Mr. Villette?" she asked, not quite able to keep the incredulity out of her voice.

"Armand Villette. Yes. Do sit down, Miss Deering, and tell me what the trouble is. My secretary gave me an incoherent story. A mystery about Aurora and something about some old woman. Shall we start with Aurora who, I might say, I was extremely sorry to lose. I understood she was getting married.".

Lydia nodded. Completely ordinary. No, not completely when one looked at him more closely. He had a way of tucking his chin into his neck and looking over the top of his glasses, showing only the whites of his eyes. It gave him a scheming, slightly macabre look that did not fit in with his relaxed appearance, his hands clasped, his body still.

"Aurora was getting married," she said. "As far as we know, she is married. But it didn't take place at home, as we had expected. Nor to the man she was engaged to."

"Good gracious!" exclaimed Mr. Villette, his eyes growing rounder than ever. "How extraordinary! Who did she marry then?"

Lydia smoothed her gloves. "We don't know. She seems to have eloped." After a moment she added, "Actually, we hoped you might be able to help."

"I? Willingly, my dear Miss Deering. But in what way? Do you want me to get this extraordinary marriage annulled? You are, perhaps, on the side of the jilted suitor?"

Lydia didn't like the flash of his eye or the faint slyness of his smile—as if he took a furtive pleasure in this kind of contretemps.

"We merely want to know the truth," she said shortly.

"Yes, of course. One understands that. Indeed, I should like to know it myself. An elopement, eh? Aurora was very attractive. She was a decoration to the office as well as being extremely efficient. But as to her private life, I knew nothing.

71

Nothing, Miss Deering." His voice was involuntarily wistful. He sighed a little. Suddenly he looked more than middle-aged, a portly, rather dull solicitor sitting in his office surrounded by files and leather-bound law books.

So this was Aurora's Armand! Lydia still couldn't quite believe it.

"You gave her a beautiful present," she murmured. "That gold pendant."

"Oh, that!" Did he hesitate a little? "But for the wrong wedding, one perceives."

No particular reaction there. Yet it had been a surprisingly tasteful and original present for such a man to choose.

"If you're asking my advice, Miss Deering, there's nothing you can do except wait for Aurora to come back. She's of age. She's obviously gone of her own free will. And she's not a girl to tolerate recriminations. So you'd better tell the rejected fiancé to find himself another girl."

"You can really tell me nothing, Mr. Villette?"

He leaned forward across the desk intimately. "What did you think I could tell you, Miss Deering?"

Lydia was confused. "I—I don't really know. But you'd seen more of Aurora than we had over the past few years. I'm only her step-sister, you know. And she'd quarrelled with my parents. We'd rather lost touch."

"A love of the dramatic, eh? She should have been on the stage. Well, now, what's this about an old woman. What has it to do with Aurora?"

"A Miss Clara Wilberforce," said Lydia, watching him.

"Yes? Who is she?"

"You don't know? You haven't heard her name before?"

"Should I have?" His thick eyebrows rose. "Are you cross-examining me, Miss Deering?"

"Of course not. I just thought Aurora would have told you about her. She's in very distressed circumstances because her sister, too, strangely enough, seems to have disappeared, though it isn't an elopement in this case. Apart from being very upset about that, it seems the sister made her a weekly allowance, and now that's stopped."

"Yes," said Mr. Villette. "Go on."

"That's all. She's been turned out of her room for not paying the rent and she's come to me—at least, to Aurora's flat. She means to go to the police if we can do nothing for her."

Mr. Villette tapped his finger tips together.

"This is all very strange and interesting, Miss Deering, but what exactly has it to do with me? In what way can I assist?"

"Didn't Aurora say anything to you? She promised Miss Wilberforce she would."

"Not a word. What was she to say?"

"Why, that Miss Wilberforce came here to see you because you used to act for her sister. She thought you might know something about her whereabouts. You were busy at the time, but Aurora apparently promised to tell you about it."

"Then I'm afraid your beautiful sister's mind has been on her own private affairs. This would perhaps be a little clearer, Miss Deering, if you can tell me the mysterious disappearing sister's name."

"It's a strange name. Blandina. Mrs. Blandina Paxton."

Mr. Villette sprang up so abruptly that Lydia was startled.

"But that's extraordinary! That's my Aunt Blandina!"

"Your aunt!"

"Yes, indeed. I took her down to my place in the country a little while ago. She hadn't been well. I at last persuaded her to leave that wretched hotel where she'd lived for years. Why, goodness me, I never knew she had a sister. Certainly not one dependent on her."

Lydia struggled with her perplexity. "Excuse me, Mr. Villette, but if Blandina—I mean Mrs. Paxton—is your aunt, isn't Miss Wilberforce also your aunt?"

"Not at all. Aunt Blandina is an aunt by marriage. She married my Uncle Paxton who died many years ago. My mother and she became close friends. We've always been very fond of her. But we never knew she had a sister, if you can believe anything so remarkable!"

"I think Miss Clara has been rather a black sheep."

"She must have been! How amusing! Well, well. One lives and learns about human nature. And I've acted for Aunt

73

Blandina for years without her breathing a word. I must do something for this unfortunate creature. What's she like?"

"Very sweet, but a little frail in her wits."

"Then I know the very thing to do. She must come down to the country to be with Aunt Blandina."

He was almost benevolent. Almost. Had his eyes been still they would have been kind. But surely he was kind to instantly propose such a perfect solution to Miss Wilberforce's troubles.

"Why, that's a wonderful idea!"

"It's the obvious one. You must tell her. Or I'll come and see her. Is she staying with you?"

Lydia nodded. "She arrived late last night. She thought she was coming to Aurora. I can't understand——"

Mr. Villette interrupted soothingly. "Don't criticise your sister, my dear. Wait until you reach that happy day yourself."

Lydia winced inwardly at his ever so slightly false benevolence.

"If it *was* a happy day," she murmured.

"Yes, well, the minx deserves a good spanking, eh?" He laughed noisily, his face red and hearty, his large, pale-blue eyes rolling.

No, Aurora, so fastidious and exquisite, could not have thought twice about a man like this. He was just Armand-and-his-aunts, a dull little motley of elderly people.

And yet her voice, when she had spoken of him, had held a caress. . . . One had been so sure. . . .

"I'm afraid I have another appointment in a few minutes, Miss Deering. Now how would it be if I dropped in at your flat this evening and met Miss Wilberforce? Did you say her name was Clara—Aunt Clara, then. I am a man with many aunts, Miss Deering. They occupy almost all of my private life, I'm afraid, but what can one do? One can't leave them to die alone, or in destitution. Anyway, if Aunt Clara seems amenable, we'll take her down to Greenhill tomorrow or the next day. It's a large house. There's plenty of room. And I'm sure Aunt Blandina will be persuaded to forgive her sister for her black sheepmanship"—his noisy laugh burst out again —"and enjoy her company."

74

"Tonight?" said Lydia. "About eight?"

"That would be excellent. I shall look forward to it. Write down the address for me, will you. I never trust my memory nowadays. I'm so glad to have met you, Miss Deering. And I'll be more than interested when news of Aurora comes along. Can you——"

"Yes, I can see myself out."

"Good. Tonight at eight then. Tell Aunt Clara to put on her best bib and tucker for her long-lost nephew."

Strangely enough, the outer office was still empty as Lydia went out, the typewriter covered, the desk neat.

"My secretary has the afternoon off," called Armand Villette after her, as if he were uncannily divining her thoughts. "To go to a wedding. That might amuse you!"

His loud laughter followed her as she went down the stairs.

But when the man in the inner office was alone he quickly shut the door, then began to mop his forehead.

"You can come out now," he said, in an exhausted voice, and the door of the small washroom behind him slowly opened.

8

It was just after noon. The long, low car pulled up at a telephone box in the suburbs and a man got out. He went round the car and opened the opposite door for his companion.

"This will do. Make it snappy."

The girl crossed the pavement and pushed open the door of the telephone box. When the man made to follow her she tried to pull the door shut in front of him.

"There's only room for one."

"No, no, plenty of room for two skinnies!" he said gaily. "Don't shut me out, darling. It's a cold wind."

"Cold! You're telling me!" she muttered. She asked for the number and waited to slide the coins into the slot.

75

She was conscious all the time of the man pressed against her back, watching and listening. Her excitement at his nearness was not excitement any longer. Or it was a different kind of excitement, devastating and dangerous.

Then Millicent's high enquiring voice answered, and she began to speak, "Mummy?" How long was it since she had called Millicent Mummy—not since she was eighteen—so why had she done so now?

"Aurora! It's not Aurora!"

"Yes, it is. Look, Mummy, I have only a minute——"

"But where are you ringing from, darling? Not Edinburgh?"

"No, not Edinburgh now."

"But you are married, darling?"

"Of course." Had she hesitated? She didn't think so. "Mummy, I'm catching a train. I truly have only a minute. Is Lydia there? I want to speak to her."

"She's not here. She's in London. She's staying in your flat, hoping you'd come back. Darling, you are going back, aren't you?"

"Not just yet. Later, of course." She felt the man prodding her elbow. "Mummy, would you give Lydia a message for me. An important message. I haven't time to put another call through now. Would you tell her that if she won't post that pendant on—you know, the one that was a wedding present, I wrote about it—would she take it to Mr. Armand Villette's office for safe keeping. Then I can pick it up when I get back to London. It's rather valuable. I don't want it lying round. Have you got that?"

"Mr. Armand Villette. What's his address?"

"34 Pyne Street, W.C.1. He's a solicitor. I used to work there. I've written him a letter explaining. Are you sure that's clear?"

"I think so, dear. But where are you now?"

"In a telephone box, and the train's just due to leave." The iron-hard hand was gripping her arm. "I have to fly."

"But, Aurora, who did you marry? You haven't told me——"

"Mummy, I'm not——" she began to say in a rush.

76

One hand went quick as a flash over her mouth. The other wrenched the receiver out of her grasp.

She looked up into his brilliant smile.

"Why did you have to do that? You beast! Oh, how I hate you!"

Tears of anger and pain filled her eyes. She moved sharply away from his intended caress. But the telephone box was narrow and she was jammed against the glass window.

"You don't really hate me, you know." His eyes were narrowed and tender, smiling, beguiling. "But we want to keep our secret a little longer, don't we? Don't we?"

She was hypnotised, as she had always been. And there seemed to be no other way anyway.

She nodded helplessly, and let him take her hand as they opened the door into the cold wind. The tears were still in her eyes.

9

"But I tell you, it's a splendid idea," Lydia insisted to Philip. "Miss Wilberforce going down to the country to be with her sister. We might have known there was a simple explanation to this silly mystery."

"You say this Villette fellow is middle-aged, not handsome."

"Far from handsome. He even looks aunt-ridden. He's the portly, unromantic middle-aged bachelor who conceals a heart of gold. How else could one explain him taking on another old woman so readily?"

"Sounds a little too ready."

"Philip! Why are you so suspicious?"

"So were you half an hour ago."

"I know, but I hadn't seen him then. I tell you, no one could be less of a Don Juan. Anyway, we don't even know he is a bachelor. He may have a wife."

"Darling, no one with all those aunts is likely to have a wife."

Lydia stopped involuntarily. They were walking on the edge of the park. The trees cast shadows like a French Impressionist painting, the grass was cucumber green.

"You called me darling," she said flatly.

"So I did. It suits you."

"Please don't again. It must be only a habit you have. You didn't ask whether I found out anything about Aurora. I didn't. Not a thing. Mr. Villette was—or seemed to be—as mystified as us. Although I don't think he thought it was an entirely unexpected thing for Aurora to do. He said she was very attractive. He asked me what I expected him to do, annul the marriage, or something?"

Philip took her arm. "You're talking too much, Lydia. Let's leave Aurora to her chosen husband, shall we? She's well able to look after herself, you know."

Lydia suddenly found his calmness infuriating and intolerable.

"How can you speak of her so objectively. You loved her, didn't you? Or if you didn't, why did you ask her to marry you?"

"She dazzled and bewitched me," Philip murmured. "I was going to have this lovely thing to paint forever. One shouldn't try to turn a dream into reality. Or should I say a ghost into a real woman?"

But his last words brought back that chilly vision of Aurora sleeping in a cobwebby bed.

Lydia began to talk vigorously. "How impractical you are! Would you really enjoy a ghost cooking for you? Ugh! Cobwebs and smoke. Let's hurry home and see what Miss Wilberforce is doing. She at least is someone real."

Miss Wilberforce had only one anxious query to make about her proposed visit to the country, "How far away was the nearest post office?"

"I'm a great letter-writer, as you know. I want access to letter-boxes and stamps. My friends would be so distressed if I stopped writing."

"Your friends?" Lydia queried, wondering where those particular people had been while Miss Wilberforce was in want.

78

"Look!" the old lady said proudly, tumbling the contents of her handbag on to the floor.

There lay scattered dozens of letters, surely the accumulation of months or years. But curiously enough almost all the envelopes, tattered and much handled, bore the same handwriting, the sprawling shaky hand of Miss Wilberforce herself.

"Well, isn't that splendid!" Lydia murmured.

"Yes, isn't it?" The old lady beamed with the greatest pleasure. "Do you know, I have discovered that if I post a letter early enough in the morning it reaches me the same day. Isn't that fascinating!"

"What do you write about?" Lydia asked, with interest.

"Oh, everything. The weather, the overseas news, the latest plays, the fashions. Oh, yes, my letters are very informative. Now do you suppose this place of my nephew is near to another village? It's the greatest fun to take a bus journey and post a letter away from home. It makes one feel one is on holiday."

"But you will be on holiday, Miss Wilberforce."

The old lady pouted a little. She didn't look particularly elated at the prospect. "With Blandina. Even as a child she was so bossy. I'm delighted she's safe, of course, but then one hardly expected anything really interesting to happen to Blandina. Well, we shall see. Perhaps I'll be able to sneak out and catch a bus now and then."

"I'll write to you myself," Lydia promised.

"Oh, my dear! Would you? But that would be tremendously exciting!"

Just before Armand Villette was due to arrive Millicent rang. Her voice was high and breathless.

"Lydia dear, I've been trying to get you. Were you out? Is everything all right? I've got the greatest news."

"What?" Lydia asked sharply.

"Aurora telephoned."

"Where from?"

"She didn't say. She hadn't time. She was catching a train. She didn't tell me anything, really, except that she wants you to take that pendant to Armand Villette's office. It's in——"

"I know all about Armand Villette," Lydia interrupted. "But is that all she told you? Just what to do with that wretched pendant?"

"Absolutely all. Isn't it maddening!"

"Well, I shouldn't worry any more about her, darling. She's just completely mercenary. I suppose this damn thing is valuable."

"Surely she can't be just thinking of its value! Unless it has a sentimental value."

"Not sentimental! I've seen Armand."

"Oh dear! How very perplexing! Actually she did begin to say something else, but she was cut off. Never mind, Lydia dear, at least we know she's safe."

Lydia refrained from pointing out that there were varying degrees of safety. She didn't know why such a thought came in her head. If Aurora had rung Millicent, even in a tearing hurry, it must have been of her own free will. She was hardly a person to be forced into anything.

There was no time to ponder on this new development nor even to tell it to Philip (who surely must be hurt afresh that Aurora had not mentioned him), for the doorbell had rung and Armand Villette was there.

He stood, portly and exuding goodwill, on the doorstep. He had a large bunch of roses which he presented to Lydia with a small bow, saying they were in appreciation of her kindness to his Aunt Blandina's sister. Then he followed Lydia into the living-room and bowed again to Miss Wilberforce who had shrunk back into the couch in a way that seemed both nervous and hostile. Like a wary elderly cat, afraid of new surroundings, not used to being uprooted.

"So this is Aunt Clara," he said in his hearty voice. "I'm so pleased to meet you. Do forgive me for never having known of your existence!"

"That's not surprising," Miss Wilberforce said bluntly. "Blandina was always ashamed of me."

"And this is Philip Nash," Lydia said, indicating Philip

who stood at the window. "Philip is—was—a friend of Aurora's."

"The jilted bridegroom," said Philip airily. "No doubt you guessed."

"Oh, dear, dear!" murmured Mr. Villette. "This rather brings that little contretemps home. I'm afraid I wasn't taking it very seriously when Miss Deering told me about it at the office. I mean, youth, impulsiveness, and so on."

"Aurora's twenty-five," Lydia said.

Philip's bland expression suggested that they were talking of someone he had known only casually, but she knew him better now. He did not indulge in a display of emotion.

"My poor dear fellow!" said Armand Villette unctuously.

"May the best man win." Philip was still airy. He held out cigarettes. "Do you smoke, Mr. Villette?"

"Thank you, no."

"Do sit down," Lydia said. "You'll want to talk to Miss Wilberforce."

Armand sat down heavily beside Miss Wilberforce, and the old lady, shrinking farther into the cushions, muttered, "Yes, she was always ashamed of me. I was a rather stupid and silly child, and of course her attitude made me much worse."

"Then we must make amends for all that now," Armand said soothingly. "Miss Deering has probably told you of my little plan. It will give me the greatest pleasure to have you at Greenhill, and I'm sure we can persuade Aunt Blandina to change her mind about you. Eh?"

Miss Wilberforce suddenly forgot her nervousness, or perhaps decided that this portly, kind man was not a person of whom to be afraid. She treated him to one of her round milky-blue stares.

"Why should you do this for me, a complete stranger?"

"Not a stranger, Aunt Clara! I won't have you calling me that." He was hearty, humorous. He almost wagged his plump forefinger. "I am a man who has had many aunts—seven, to be exact—and frankly I adored them all. Now I have only two left—Aunt Honoria, who lives in Brittany (she belongs to the French side of the family), and Aunt Blandina."

81

"What has happened to the others?" Miss Wilberforce enquired.

"Oh, passed away, I fear."

Miss Wilberforce's stare went milkier, and Armand said a little uncomfortably, "One grows old, you know. I'm fifty-one myself."

"I'm seventy-four," said Miss Wilberforce. "Blandina is seventy-six. Is she failing?"

"Naturally, a little. Her memory mostly."

"Then that's why she forgot my allowance."

"I'm afraid so. Otherwise she'd surely have told me when I decided to move her to Greenhill. She wasn't fit to stay on at that hotel alone. And if it comes to that, my dear Aunt Clara——"

"I'm perfectly fit!" Miss Wilberforce declared. "I am not yet to be one of your 'passed away' aunts."

"Not for a very long time," Armand assured her in tones of horror.

"Not living in the country in comfort," Lydia put in.

Armand flashed her what seemed to be, strangely enough, a look of gratitude. As if he had expected trouble and was glad of her co-operation.

Miss Wilberforce tossed her head peevishly. "I'm not at all sure that I want to go into the country with a complete stranger. I have no nephews, after all."

"But, Aunt Clara——"

"It's very late in the day, in my seventy-fifth year, to present yourself, nephew Armand!"

"But don't you understand, I didn't know about you. If I had known——"

"What would you have done? Buried me in your country house, away from post offices and other amenities."

Armand looked blank, and Lydia explained as tactfully as possible Miss Wilberforce's small eccentricity about writing and receiving letters.

"Oh, I see. That's simply arranged. The village post office is half a mile away, but we have our mail collected at the house. Nothing could be easier."

82

"But that's cheating!" Miss Wilberforce exclaimed indignantly. "One goes *out* to post a letter."

"My dear aunt——" Armand patted her hand. "That can all be arranged when you arrive. Now what do you say to tomorrow morning. I'll call for you in my car at eleven o'clock. It's only two hours' run. Very pleasant on a fine day."

Miss Wilberforce shook her head, suddenly stubborn.

"I find I don't care for the idea, after all. To stagnate in the country until I pass away. Blandina may not mind that idea, but I most definitely do."

"Aunt Clara——" Armand looked shocked, and was, for once, without words.

Lydia looked at Philip, who had been watching silently, then she sat beside the old lady and said, "Dear Miss Wilberforce, everyone has to die, but you're not going to for years. Mr. Villette is only trying to help you. He says you'll be very comfortable, and you will be with your own sister. After all, what can happen to you in London? Much as I'd like to, I can't keep you very long because this isn't even my own flat. It's Aurora's, and she won't be able to have you here when she comes back with a new husband." She noticed, out of the corner of her eye, Armand Villette's curious gaze going over the room and she knew, all at once, that he had never been in it before. His gaze stopped at the Monet over the mantelpiece, and became narrowed with speculation.

"I think you'll really have to go and give it a trial, you know," she went on. "If you hate it, perhaps you can persuade your sister to start your allowance again. But I really don't think you should go on living alone."

"Passed away, indeed!" snorted Miss Wilberforce.

"An unfortunate phrase," Armand murmured.

Miss Wilberforce suddenly gripped Lydia's hand. "I'll go if you'll come with me."

"Come with you!" She was aware, more than anything, of Armand's startled gaze. "He doesn't want me to come," she thought. "I wonder why?"

"Yes. Come and see if this woman is really my sister

83

Blandina," Miss Wilberforce said eagerly. "I haven't seen her for so long, I may not even know her again."

"But Miss Deering has never seen her at all," Armand pointed out. "That really solves nothing, Aunt Clara."

Philip, watching, said nothing. Nor did his expression tell anything. He, Lydia thought, should have been playing Armand's part, if Armand really had something to conceal.

"Please come, Lydia dear," Miss Wilberforce pleaded. "I can't travel alone with a completely strange man. It would hardly be right."

"My *dear* Aunt Clara——"

Lydia, interrupting Armand, said clearly, as if she had abruptly changed her mind, "All right. I'll come. That will be all right, won't it, Mr. Villette? If it makes Miss Wilberforce happier. I can get her settled and catch a train back to London."

"Certainly, if you insist," Armand agreed stiffly. He could do nothing else. But his eyes were restless again. He looked at his hands, and then at Lydia. "It is quite unnecessary, you know. I don't want to take up your time, and I'm sure Aunt Clara wouldn't if she realised how unnecessary it was."

"Oh, I shall enjoy it," Lydia said blithely. "And I'd love to meet your Aunt Blandina. She seems, if you don't mind my saying so, something of a myth."

"No myth about her," Armand muttered, and suddenly Lydia knew something else—that his Aunt Blandina was not his favourite aunt. Then was he being a good nephew because of her money?

"I shall only stay if Lydia thinks it is all right," Miss Wilberforce declared, in her deep dramatic voice. "I trust her. Oh, don't think I'm slighting you, nephew Armand. But I don't know you, do I? I've never set eyes on you before."

When Armand had gone, making his deliberate pompous way down the stairs, June Birch presented herself. She came in with her brash assurance and nodded to Philip.

"He's not the one, duck. He definitely wasn't her type."

"What do you mean?" Lydia demanded.

"I was just settling a small point." Philip explained coolly. "I asked June to keep an eye out for our expected visitor and see whether she recognised him."

"Oh, Armand hadn't been here before," Lydia said. "I knew that by the way he looked round this room. And that reminds me—never mind just now. Have a drink, June?"

"Love one, duck. I say, are you going to be stuck with——" She tilted her head significantly towards Miss Wilberforce, who had gone into one of her gentle blank stares.

"No, she's leaving tomorrow. We've got that sorted out. She's a connection by marriage with Armand Villette. You know, I can't think why Aurora didn't straighten that out. She can never have taken time to mention the poor old thing to Armand."

"Guess her own affairs were needing all her straightening powers," June said cynically. Philip handed her a drink and she added, "Here's the skin off your nose."

"I expect I ought to pack," observed Miss Wilberforce, who had no possessions at all except her bulging handbag, and the few toilet articles Lydia had given her. "I believe this *is* rather exciting after all. I haven't had a trip to the country for so long. The may will be out. And you will write to me, Lydia dear."

"Miss Wilberforce adores getting letters," Lydia explained to June.

"Do you, duck. Bless you, then we'll all write to you." When June had gone and Miss Wilberforce had courteously excused herself to pack and to attend to "urgent correspondence" Philip said to Lydia, "And what were you reminded of a little while ago? I don't like half-finished sentences."

"Oh, that. I didn't particularly want June to hear. It's just that I can't understand Aurora's concern over that pendant which can't be a quarter as valuable as that picture, for instance. She goes away leaving her flat keys about almost indiscriminately, and yet fusses about a piece of jewellery."

"I expect the picture is well-insured and the pendant isn't. What about the pendant, anyway? Has something more come up?"

So then Lydia had to watch his face as she told him of Aurora's telephone call.

"Was that absolutely all she said?" he asked at last.

"Millicent says so. Aurora was catching a train and in a hurry."

"A convenient hurry?"

"Oh, I don't know, Philip."

His eyes narrowed. "She becomes a dream, the lovely Aurora. It's a pity she's still dependent on mundane things like trains. One imagines her spreading wings, like a moth. Or something less innocent and helpless, perhaps. A night-time bird. An owl. Or a bat."

Then his eyes flew open and shone with their sudden disconcerting intensity. "I apologise for that whimsicality. Even bats don't wear antique gold pendants. Are you going to deliver it to Armand Villette?"

"What do you think? If I had been going to I'd have given it to him tonight."

"Stubborn little sister, aren't you? Give it to me, will you?"

"Why?"

"Just a matter of curiosity. I'd like to take it to a jeweller and find out its value."

"What will that serve to explain?"

"Something, I should think. If it's worth five thousand pounds we know for certain Aurora is merely mercenary. But if it's only worth a fiver, which I strongly suspect is more its mark, we only have one other explanation. That it has deep sentimental value. Candidly, do you think it has?"

"As a present from the pompous Armand!" Lydia said incredulously.

"You see what I mean?"

Lydia shook her head slowly. "I'm sure of one thing only, and that's that he didn't want me to go down with him tomorrow."

"He isn't the only one with those sentiments."

"You!" Lydia exclaimed in surprise.

"Bless your kind heart, Lydia dear, but you've done enough

86

for your stray old woman without getting involved with a shady solicitor."

"Do you think he's shady?"

"Didn't you decide yourself that he was a little too plausible? Everything fitting in, like a jigsaw puzzle. Everything, that is, except Aurora. And one couldn't, even by the longest stretch of imagination, see them as lovers. Unless it were for gold pendants. . . ."

"Philip, don't be absurd! Aurora used to talk about Armand and his aunts. You said so yourself. None of this is really in the least unexpected. Anyway, what could he want with a penniless old creature like Miss Wilberforce? And he certainly wouldn't take me down tomorrow if there were no Blandina. Would he?"

Philip raised an eyebrow.

"All right. Have it your own way. Armand is a nice, plump, sentimental philanthropist, and Miss Wilberforce is being put into a comfortable pasture for her old age. After all, it's nothing to do with us, is it? We don't want to get as poky-nosed as June Birch. Damned boring. Now I'll go and look up train timetables."

"Why?" Lydia felt stupid and a step behind him all the time.

"To see what train you'll come back on tomorrow. And," he added sternly, "you be sure you're on it!"

10

Philip tapped at the receptionist's desk in the hotel. A middle-aged woman appeared from an office at the back.

"Good morning, sir. Can I help you?"

She looked overwhelmingly respectable. Indeed, the whole place did: drab, comfortable, genteel, infinitely depressing.

"I hope you can," he said. "I've just arrived in London from a long absence abroad and I'm looking for an elderly relative.

87

This is the last address I have of hers. Could you possibly tell me anything about her? Mrs. Paxton. Mrs. Blandina Paxton."

"Oh, I am sorry, sir, you're just too late. She left here—let me see—a few weeks ago. I can give you the exact date if you like. She'd been here for years, too."

Philip made a suitable exclamation of disappointment.

"Now isn't that bad luck. Can you tell me where she went?"

"No, I can't, sir. I vaguely think it was Bournemouth. Her nephew took her away. At least, I guessed it was her nephew because he called her aunt. You'd know who I'd mean, perhaps."

Philip nodded.

"Then you can get in touch with him, can't you? We were sorry to lose Mrs. Paxton. She'd been here nearly twenty years, you know. The oldest inhabitant. But she was failing, poor old dear. Her memory was going. We were glad to see someone belonging to her turn up."

"You mean this nephew didn't usually visit her?"

"I can't really say, sir. I haven't been here long. And she always went out, you know, to tea or the cinema, the way old ladies do. He might have visited or she might have met him. But you can trace him, can't you?"

"Yes. Certainly."

"If it helps at all, he came in a Jaguar. Oh, and there was a girl. His wife, I expect."

The woman looked at him with a friendly smile, wondering if the conversation were completed.

"She moved all her things?" Philip asked.

"Mrs. Paxton? Oh, yes. Mr. Seagar's in her room now. But he won't last twenty years, I'm afraid. It's heart with him. Oh, by the way, there has been someone enquiring for Mrs. Paxton. A rather pathetic old creature who said she was her sister. She seemed upset not to find her. But Mrs. Paxton never mentioned a sister to anyone here. She never mentioned any relatives. We thought she was alone in the world until this nephew and his wife turned up."

"What did they look like?" Philip asked casually. "I just want to be sure which of my many cousins they would have been."

"Well, I didn't really see the girl. She stayed in the car. She had dark hair. The man wore dark glasses. He wasn't exactly good-looking but he had such a way with him. He only had to smile. Even I noticed that!"

The woman coloured slightly and remembered her dignity. "That's all I can tell you, sir."

"Thank you very much," said Philip. "You've been very kind."

From Bayswater Philip caught a bus to Bloomsbury. He found the office of Armand Villette without difficulty. He knew Armand was away for the day, dealing with yet another aunt. It was perfectly safe to go in without encountering him, and to get an impression of his office, and his secretary. To see the place where Aurora had worked, but to which she had never let him come. Perhaps to ask some pertinent questions. He was by no means satisfied about Armand Villette. The man was too plausible. And he had not yet seen him exhibit the charm that the receptionist at the Bayswater hotel talked about.

Yet what was there to put a finger on?

He obviously hadn't been Aurora's lover, and the old lady, Aunt Blandina, must be at his home in Sussex, otherwise he could not have risked Lydia going down.

If only one could find Aurora. . . .

But did he now want to find her? Wasn't he secretly relieved about the whole thing—except for her haunting beauty, which had first eluded him on canvas and now in reality.

Hadn't he begun to wake up from that bemused dream the moment he met Lydia on Waterloo station and thought, "Here's someone I can talk to."

If Lydia came back today and reported that all was well, that Blandina had welcomed her sister, and Miss Wilberforce had settled down happily, one would be tempted to dismiss the whole matter from one's mind, to plunge into work and forget this brief spring madness.

Yet here he was on his way to Armand Villette's office to take the opportunity of doing a little snooping. He wanted to

89

talk with the secretary who probably had known Aurora. He hadn't met Aurora's friends. There hadn't been time. Wait until she had left work, she had said, and then, wait until they were married.

It seemed he wasn't to meet anyone today, either, for the door into Armand Villette's suite of offices was locked.

After he had tried the knob and knocked in vain, an elderly charwoman who had been cleaning the entrance hall called up the stairs, "There's no one there today. They're shut."

Philip came down the stairs. "I know Mr. Villette's away, but hasn't he a secretary?"

The woman came out of the shadowy part of the hall to look up at him. She gave a cackle of laughter. "She got the sack, that one!"

"Which one?"

"Why, the one that was here last week. Not the dark one who left to get married. She was all right. She'd been here a long time. No, the one that started last week. Didn't last long, did she?"

"Apparently not," Philip murmured.

"So that's why the office is locked up today. No one to look after it. I'd call again tomorrow, if I was you. Be back then, I should think."

The woman, fat and phlegmatic and not particularly interested, except in her brief maliciousness about the dismissed secretary, waddled off to her brooms and buckets.

Philip, too, had no alternative but to go. He had got nowhere, and did not know whether or not to place any significance in the secretary's dismissal. A week would have proved whether or not she was competent. It may genuinely have been a matter of incompetence.

Now he had only one matter left to attend to. He went into a jeweller's shop that showed a notice "Secondhand jewellery bought", and produced the antique gold pendant.

The man behind the counter studied it closely through a magnifying glass. He looked up, with shrewd bargaining eyes.

"It's quite a nice piece, sir. Early Victorian, I would say. But there's no market for it. The diamonds aren't first quality and the ruby has a flaw. I couldn't offer more than twenty-five pounds for it."

"That's a genuine offer?"

"Certainly." The man was slightly offended. "You can take it somewhere else. You can have it valued a dozen times. But you'll find I'm not far out."

"Thank you," said Philip, pocketing the pendant, "I'll think about it."

He walked out of the shop into the cool spring sunlight. So it was sentiment and not greed that Aurora felt. Sentiment about Armand Villette, with his round, pale-blue eyes showing their whites above his spectacles?

Suddenly, for no apparent reason, he was wishing the day were over and Lydia back.

11

The house was, as Armand had said, about half a mile from the village. It was approached by a long drive bordered by thick shrubs, and came into view only when one virtually burst upon it at the last turn of the drive. It was a large, two-storey building of grey stone, well-kept and attractive. Gardens, bright with tulips and apple blossom, stretched to both sides.

It was no run-down old women's home, but the estate of someone who enjoyed tasteful living. It looked as if Miss Wilberforce had fallen very firmly on her feet. This thought had apparently come to Miss Wilberforce, too, for she was smiling with pleasure and exclaiming,

"Isn't this grand! Do you really live here, nephew Armand? Does being a solicitor pay for all this?"

Armand gave his loose-lipped smile. His face had its usual genial look, but the whites of his eyes were showing over the top of his spectacles again, with that suggestion of hidden anxiety.

"I have a little money, you know, Aunt Clara. But Aunt

Blandina will give you all my family history. Come along in. She's expecting you."

Lydia got out of the car and felt Miss Wilberforce grip her arm nervously.

"Oh dear! Is she annoyed with me for coming here? She'll feel I'm intruding, of course."

"Nonsense, Aunt Clara. Look at all these empty rooms." Armand waved towards the row of windows. "I could keep a dozen guests here very easily."

He led the way up the steps, through the white Queen Anne door, into a spacious hall.

The carpets were soft, the curtains rich and tasteful, the few ornaments and pictures obviously of value. Even more in here than outside there was an air of unostentatious wealth. In spite of herself Lydia was impressed. No one who lived like this could need to have designs on an old woman.

Yet a niggling doubt remained in her mind. Armand Villette, genial, a little plump, just vaguely shambling, not particularly erudite, as the desultory conversation during the two-hour journey had proved, did not fit in here. It did not seem at all possible that the mind responsible for the taste and graciousness of this house could have been his.

The front door had been unlocked. No one came forward to meet them. Armand, in his diffident way, suggested that before lunch Miss Wilberforce should go upstairs and see her room and then have a few words with her sister who was confined to her bed. He turned apologetically to Lydia and said, "Perhaps you wouldn't mind waiting down here. Aunt Blandina is not at all well. The doctor says as few visitors as possible. I think the meeting with her long-lost sister will be all she can cope with just at present. There's a cloakroom through this door. And then perhaps you would like to wait in the drawing-room."

"But I'll get to see Aunt Blandina before I leave," Lydia told herself as she washed and renewed her make-up in the cloak-room. There was no necessity to see the old woman, of course. Nothing could be more highly respectable than this house, and in any case Miss Wilberforce, an acquaintance of forty-eight hours, should be no concern of hers. Beyond the way a stray cat would be. Though actually she felt rather strongly about all stray creatures, and it had become important to see that Miss Wilberforce, with her mild blue eyes and crumpled cheeks, was happy.

Ten minutes later Armand came downstairs. He said, "Ah, now, a little drink before luncheon. Aunt Clara will be down shortly. The two old dears, bless them, are having a wonderful reunion. What will you have, Miss Deering? Can I mix you a martini? I do them very well." The whites of his eyes peered coyly over his glasses.

"Thank you," said Lydia politely. "What a lovely room this is."

"Yes, isn't it?" His voice was absent as he mixed drinks.

"And a lovely garden," said Lydia at the window, watching a tall young man mowing the lawns. "You're lucky to have a gardener."

"Eh? Oh, the gardener! That's Jules. Yes, I am lucky. He works hard."

What had he thought she had said? Lydia wondered. He had seemed startled.

"And he's young," she commented. "Usually gardeners nowadays are nursing their stiff joints."

"Jules is devoted to his work." Armand dismissed the gardener, and handing her a drink said, "Tell me if this is to your liking."

She sipped it with pleasure. She had needed it, and was at last beginning to relax. The journey was over. Miss Wilberforce had arrived. That strange episode, vaguely linked with the mystery of Aurora, was satisfactorily explained and ended. Aurora, also, would shortly turn up to explain her behaviour. All was well. And Philip was meeting her train this evening. . . .

"Is it all right, Miss Deering?" came Armand's voice. He peered at her over his glasses, an anxious, slightly shambling middle-aged man, so kind as to become aunt-ridden, beautifully uncomplaining about a new claimant on his generosity. How could she have thought he was even vaguely sinister?

"It's very good indeed."

"Fine. There'll be time for another before Aunt Clara comes down. Well, this is an unexpectedly pleasant day." So Armand, too, was beginning to relax. But why had he needed to?

Lydia sipped her drink and watched the gardener moving slowly back and forth with the lawn-mower. He seemed to glance towards the windows occasionally as if in his turn he were watching her. But she couldn't be sure of that. The drink was making her fanciful.

"Did you ever bring Aurora down here?" she asked.

"Your sister? Yes. Actually she came the day I brought Aunt Blandina. History repeats itself, eh?"

He gave his thick-lipped smile, and his ingenuous glance, and Lydia said casually, "Was your Aunt Blandina the one Aurora mentioned? She said something about a car accident."

For a split second she saw his look of uncertainty, bafflement. Then he answered smoothly enough, "That was Aunt Honoria who was over for a visit just before Christmas. She lives in Brittany. Aurora was good enough to do things for her."

"You must miss Aurora," Lydia murmured.

"I certainly do, Miss Deering. I certainly do."

Lydia strolled round the room. "You have some wonderful pictures. Aurora has a Monet, you know."

"Only a copy, I'm afraid. She mentioned it when she bought it." But yesterday he had looked hard at that picture as if he had never seen it before, as if it being there on Aurora's wall had startled him. . . .

Lydia couldn't concentrate. The drink was making her extraordinarily limp and muddled. It must have been very strong. Deliberately strong? So she couldn't concentrate, wouldn't notice too much?

The tall gardener moved slowly back and forth in the sunlight, the colours in the garden blurred. . . .

"I'll just bring Aunt Clara down to luncheon," Armand said behind her. "Wait there."

Wait there! Why? Because he didn't want her to open any forbidden doors? The hall, the impersonal cloakroom, the lovely long drawing-room with its carefully chosen treasures,

94

presently the dining-room. . . . That was all she was to be allowed to see.

But no! She was going to see Aunt Blandina. She had determined on that.

Armand came back, leading Miss Wilberforce. The old lady seemed to look bewildered and distressed. Or was that, too, her imperfect vision? Lydia shook her head impatiently, trying to clear it. Why had she weakly consented to drinking Armand's crafty martini when she could have had a simple sherry?

"I've been talking to Blandina," Miss Wilberforce was saying. "And Armand has given me a beautiful room. Such luxury. I don't know."

"What don't you know?" Armand asked genially. "Come this way. It's only a cold luncheon, I'm afraid. Wednesday is cook's day off."

So no one was about. The table in the panelled dining-room was set with everything necessary—cold meats, salad, rolls, a piled dish of fruit.

"Was your sister as you remembered her?" Lydia asked.

"Not at all. At least, I can't be sure." Miss Wilberforce frowned, seeking an elusive memory. "It's so long, of course, and she's changed, just as she says I have. But she always had such a loud voice. She was so bossy. Now she's quite gentle. It's so strange. Somehow I don't know."

"People change," Lydia murmured from her fog.

"You must remember Aunt Blandina is ill," Armand said. "She's lost a great deal of her aggressiveness. Oh, yes, I too know how aggressive she used to be. But she's charmed to see you, Aunt Clara. I told you she would be."

"I was never good with strangers," Miss Wilberforce muttered.

"Don't be foolish, she isn't a stranger. She's your sister."

"After twenty years she's a stranger," Miss Wilberforce insisted stubbornly. "Oh, yes, in spite of the allowance she used to send me, but that was impersonal, you understand, like receiving it from the Government, or something. Anyway, Lydia shall tell me what she thinks."

Armand, pouring wine into glasses, said, "Lydia has to catch a train after lunch, Aunt Clara. You know that. We can't take up her time indefinitely."

"Yes, of course, I know that. But not before she meets Blandina. You want to meet my sister, don't you, Lydia?"

"Indeed I do. And no wine, thank you, Mr. Villette. You must give me your special recipe for martinis. They would be a knock-out at a party."

He gave her his quick, secretive glance over the top of his spectacles.

"It wasn't a special recipe, Miss Deering. Merely the normal quantities. You probably need some food. And we must watch the time for your train."

In spite of everything being so pleasant, a luxurious house, a sunny garden, good food, he didn't want her to linger, he didn't want her to see anything except through a haze of alcohol. If she got to see Aunt Blandina, the old lady would be just another old lady in bed, cossetted, pampered, waiting to die.

It was Aunt Clara's stubbornness that brought about the meeting. She simply stated, after lunch, that now she was taking Lydia up to see Blandina, and when Armand looked fussily at his watch she said, with sudden authoritativeness, "Oh, put that away, Armand. If Lydia misses this train she catches the next. What are you worrying about? Come along, Lydia."

There was a grandfather clock in the passage outside Blandina's room. It had a deep, measured tick-tock that, to the sick old woman, must have seemed a deliberate counting away of her remaining days and hours.

But she was not a woman to be disturbed by time passing, Lydia saw at once. Although her nightgown showed her withered neck, and the scooped hollows of age at the base of her throat, and her grey hair straggled with exaggerated untidiness on the pillow, nothing could take away the vigorousness from her long nose and brilliant black eyes. One day her eyes would close and that arrogant aggressive light would go out of her face, but her long nose, poking heavenwards, would still defy mortality.

Yes. One could see the remnants of Aunt Blandina's bossy youth. And one felt there was a deliberate glossing over of that bossiness now. Miss Wilberforce had not noticed it because the voice Blandina used was deceptively gentle. But there it was, in the autocratic old face, angry at having to lie on a pillow, frantically jealous of and ready to hurl insults at those still able to walk about.

"Blandina, dear, this is Lydia. The nice girl I told you about. She has been so wonderfully kind to me."

"My dear, how good of you," came the weak, deceptively soft voice from the bed. "I've been so ill. Armand brought me here from that horrible hotel where I was all alone, and I just forgot all about poor Clara's money. I'm so ashamed."

"Now, don't fret about that, Blandina," Miss Wilberforce said. "I've been all right, thanks to Lydia, and now to Armand. You always did very well for yourself, didn't you, Blandina? First a wealthy husband and then this amazingly kind nephew!"

"Yes. I've been fortunate. But you could have been, too, Clara, if you hadn't always been such a fool. We quarrelled, you know," she explained to Lydia, her sharp eyes seeming to burn into Lydia's face. "I'm not the forgiving kind, usually. I wasn't even very pleased when Armand told me Clara was coming. But when one knows one's days are numbered, well, then. . . ." The weak voice faltered.

Clara clutched at her bony hand. "Blandina dear, you'll be all right. I'll be here now. I'll sit with you and read to you. I read quite well, you know. It's my training. Do you remember how when we were children you always wanted those soppy romances, and I wanted nothing but poetry?"

Blandina's eyes flickered open and shut.

"I haven't the faintest recollection of anything, Clara, except that you were always a perfectly detestable child, mooning, dramatising yourself." She smiled faintly, but her eyes did not soften. They were set in their beady brilliance. "But that's all over long ago. Dear me, all those years in that dreary hotel in Bayswater. Tell me, is this child staying long?"

"No, she has to catch a train. Armand is fussing."

"Then we mustn't keep her, Clara." She held out a feeble hand. "Goodbye, my dear. Forgive my not getting up. But I'm very weak after this attack. Don't miss your train. And I hope my nephew has thanked you for your care of my sister."

"I don't want thanks," Lydia said stiffly. She already disliked the old woman in the bed. She found herself hoping, for Miss Wilberforce's sake, that she did not live long, that soon Miss Wilberforce would be the loved and cosseted surviving aunt.

But there it was. She couldn't interfere. And Miss Wilberforce's future was secured.

Afterwards she wasn't able to remember the details of the bedroom very well. The curtains had been drawn, she remembered, and the room dim. The light may have tried the old woman's eyes, but they had looked too bright and unquenchable and inquisitive for any light to be too strong for them. One was left only with the picture of her untidy grey head on the pillow, her up-thrusting nose and her busy, watchful eyes. Aunt Blandina had come to rest in a comfortable spot, and so, indeed, had the vague, charming, haphazard, forgetful Clara Wilberforce.

But one did wonder why a man would welcome two distinctly eccentric old women of uncertain memory to a home on which he had clearly lavished great care.

Blandina was wealthy, of course. But Clara was not. Blandina was ill, and Clara presumably in fairly good health. It looked, on the surface, as if Clara had the best of it in all ways.

Lydia pushed the niggling doubts out of her mind and said goodbye.

"I'll write to you," she promised Miss Wilberforce. "And you be sure to write to me."

"Oh, I will," the old lady answered eagerly. "I shall be looking for your letters. Did you notice a post office in the village, by the way?"

"Yes, there is one," Armand put in. "But it's quite a walk. You only have to leave your letters in the hall, Aunt Clara, and they'll be posted."

"I enjoy a walk," murmured Miss Wilberforce, pouting a little. "It's much more fun. Even a little bus ride, now and then."

"We'll see," said Armand affably, patting her shoulder. "Jules is going to drive you to the station, Miss Deering, so I'll say goodbye. And thank you again for your help."

The Jaguar was drawn up outside the door. The tall gardener, dressed in pullover and corduroy trousers, stood waiting. He gave a quick glance at Lydia as she got into the car, then closed the door after her and slid into the driving seat.

The car moved off down the curving drive, and Lydia found herself studying the back of the driver's neck, reflecting that it was a good deal more attractive than Armand's. The neatly cut but luxuriant dark hair curled slightly at the ends, the ears were set flat, and the head held arrogantly. He may, she reflected, be a good gardener, but he was not a humble man, and as the thought passed through her head she caught his eyes in the driving mirror, strangely opaque blue eyes staring into her mirrored face unwaveringly.

For some strange reason she was embarrassed and disconcerted. It almost looked as if he were trying to tell her something. But he didn't speak, and it was left to her to open a stiff little conversation. "You're Mr. Villette's chauffeur as well as his gardener?"

"At times, madam."

She realised she had wanted to hear his voice, but the brief answer told her almost nothing. His tone was impersonal and correct. Had there been the slightest trace of a foreign accent?

"I expect he's a good employer. He's so kind to his elderly aunts."

"Yes, madam."

The grave, correct voice was completely at variance with that cold, blue, almost impertinent stare. Lydia was suddenly angry. She wasn't cross-examining him. She only wanted him to talk. But he obviously wasn't going to, and they were almost at the station, anyway.

In a few moments Jules had drawn the car up and leapt out. "You have seven minutes to wait for your train, madam."

"Thank you, Jules. I'll go on to the platform. Don't wait. Goodbye."

He stood very erect. His eyes were fixed on some spot beyond her head. He only looked at her direct in the mirror. He was not a person at all, but an image in a glass.

Even less than Miss Wilberforce and the frightening old woman in bed was he any concern of hers. She was glad to see the car move away.

If the train had not been ten minutes late she would not have got her crazy idea. But waiting restlessly on the sunny platform, smelling the country scents of trees in fresh leaf and fields of deep, thick grass, she had time to analyse her visit to Greenhill and to reflect on how unsatisfactory it had been.

She had had Armand at her elbow for the entire time except for the brief interval in the cloakroom, and later when Miss Wilberforce took her up to see her sister. There had been no servant except the gardener in sight. In a house so well-cared-for there must be several servants. Certainly Armand had said it was the cook's day off, but the cook did not keep all those rooms swept and polished. Someone else surely could have waited on the table. It must have been that Armand wanted her to see as few people as possible. He had even tried to keep her from meeting his Aunt Blandina.

On the other hand he had not minded the gardener acting as chauffeur and taking her to the station. That could have been because he had other urgent business on hand, of course.

But if so, what would it be?

Really, she had achieved absolutely nothing, and she could not be in the least certain that it was right to leave Miss Wilberforce, an elderly and helpless woman, trusting and slightly feeble in her mind, in that completely strange house. Even with her own sister who was, after all, a sister who had showed hostility and a cold charity to her all her life.

Miss Wilberforce, who had landed, like a stray, elderly child, on her doorstep, was no concern of hers, she told herself firmly. Yet why had she not been allowed to see any more of the

100

house? Why had no servants been visible? Why had Armand mixed that too strong drink? Why had the old lady in the bed stared at her like some hostile old bird?

A railway porter walked down the platform and, on an impulse, Lydia asked him the time of the next train.

"Seven-fifteen, miss."

"Thank you," said Lydia. She smiled and added, "That will suit me very well."

So she had three hours to walk back to Greenhill, to snoop about in the dusk, and then to come back to the station to catch the train. It would do very nicely indeed.

She had tea in the village. She found the post office and chatted to the postmistress, a garrulous spinster who promised to look out for Miss Wilberforce and see that her correspondence was attended to. She said it was nice that someone was living at Greenhill again as it was empty a good deal. She understood that Mr. Villette had a busy practice in London and had not much time to come down unless he had one of his aunts staying. Then, of course, he made the journey frequently. It was a pity the house hadn't a mistress, but in a way the elderly aunts provided that. The arrangement seemed to suit Mr. Villette very well.

"Does the gardener come from the village?" Lydia asked.

"Not that I know of, dear. Mr. Villette usually brings his staff with him when he comes, that is for a stay of any length. It would be some London person, I expect."

"Have many of Mr. Villette's aunts died down here?" Lydia asked casually.

"Died! Oh, no, dear! Whatever gave you that idea? I don't know of any that have died, and I've been here eleven years come Whitsun. Come to think of it, I don't think there's ever been a death at Greenhill. Not in Mr. Villette's time, anyway. Before that, of course, there was the previous owner who died and that's when Mr. Villette bought the property. Goodness, no, the old ladies stay, and then go back to their own homes, or that's what I've always thought."

"Unless they haven't homes of their own," Lydia pointed out. "Then they'd have to stay, wouldn't they? To die?"

"Well, I suppose so. But that's rather morbid, isn't it?"

By that time, with tea and the conversation with the post-mistress over, it was early dusk. Lydia left the village and set off to walk briskly up the narrow country road to the house she had left some time before.

The big gates were still open. She started up the drive, keeping close to the edge of the shrubbery, ready to take cover, if necessary. This plan proved extremely prudent, for on the last curve there was suddenly the sound of a car, and Lydia had only time to throw herself into a rhododendron bush before the big Jaguar appeared. It nosed its way slowly down the narrow drive.

Because of its lighted interior Lydia was able to see quite clearly who was in it. Armand Villette at the wheel and Jules, the gardener, beside him. The two men were conversing earnestly. Armand's head was tilted a little towards Jules worriedly. Jules, Lydia noticed, was dressed as if for the city in a dark suit, and with his hair slicked down. He was talking to Armand as if he were relating something. The arrogance in the lift of his head which Lydia had noticed earlier was even more pronounced.

She found, when the car had disappeared, that she was trembling. It had come so suddenly and she had just escaped observation. But now luckily the way was clear. She could get as close as possible to the house without stumbling into Jules working in the garden, or Armand.

Although it was still not dark there were lights showing in the big house now, one in the drawing-room windows and two others upstairs in rooms situated a little distance from each other. One, Lydia imagined, was Miss Wilberforce's and the other Blandina's.

But no. She was wrong. For as, keeping close to the gloom of the bushes, she came nearer to the house she saw a woman's figure moving in the drawing-room. It was a tall figure, moving slowly but with authority. The cook, in that long dark-coloured gown? One of the maids, previously unseen?

Lydia gave a suppressed gasp of surprise. It was Blandina. For as she stared the figure moved close to the window and looked out. There was no mistaking the long nose, the piercing black eyes. For a moment she stood quite still, her grey hair smoothly bound on the top of her head, her face brooding.

Then abruptly she lifted one of the strong bony hands that Lydia had last seen lying feebly on the coverlet of her bed and pulled the curtains across. The light was shut in. Blandina, no longer on her death bed, was enclosed with it.

Lydia was out in the dark.

12

Philip grabbed her arm as she came through the barrier.

"For heaven's sake, what happened? Why weren't you on the other train?"

"Philip, you haven't waited three hours!"

It was the first time she had seen him angry. It made his face brilliantly alive. Abruptly her tiredness and her vague anxiety and perplexity slipped away. Nothing at this moment existed but his hand gripping her arm painfully and his eyes, darkened with anger and strain, looking fiercely down at her.

This also was the first time that he had seemed to be fully alive since Aurora had left him. Her feeling of excited happiness made it difficult to be suitably apologetic for her impulsive and thoughtless behaviour.

"I didn't *wait* three hours," he said impatiently. "I went away and came back. I did think you might have missed the earlier train, but I also imagined other things."

"What?" Lydia asked interestedly. "That Armand locked me up, or something? He wouldn't have dared to do that when he knew you would be waiting for me. Anyway, he didn't want to, I assure you. He wanted to get rid of me as quickly as possible."

"Why?"

"I don't know, except that Blandina isn't as ill as she pretended to be. She began to walk about the house as soon as

103

Armand had gone. I'll tell you as we go. It is nice of you to meet me."

"You don't deserve it."

"I know. I'm growing as scatter-brained as Aurora."

"She isn't scatter-brained. She's quite the opposite. Deep and devious."

"If she's deep and devious," said Lydia slowly, "*and* mercenary, she'll come back for that Monet, as well as the gold pendant."

"She isn't that mercenary, because the pendant isn't particularly valuable."

"Oh! Did you find out?"

He nodded. "Of course, there's the chance Aurora doesn't know its real value. But I'm more inclined to think it has some other significance. What, I don't know."

"Not sentimental?"

"With Armand Villette?" he said sceptically. "And besides, she hasn't got in touch with him, or he tells us so. Anyway, tell me what happened today."

When he had heard it all, Philip said that now their responsibility, if it had ever existed, had ended. Lydia had made the journey with Miss Wilberforce to see if Blandina really existed, and, as she had discovered, she did. Now Blandina had taken over the care of her sister, as was right, and whether she exaggerated her illness or not, it was no business of theirs.

"I suppose it isn't," Lydia agreed reluctantly. "Armand made that very plain. And after all, as you say, Miss Wilberforce is with her sister. But if she writes and says she isn't happy I am going to do something about it. I'll go back and demand to see her, whether you approve or not."

"Will you?" said Philip. "I believe you will, too. You seem to be as reckless as your sister." He glanced at her thoughtfully, then, as they had come into a comparatively dark street, he suddenly pulled her into his arms and kissed her.

It was a fierce kiss that seemed to be expressing his anger and hurt over Aurora more than desire for Lydia. After a startled and ecstatic moment Lydia pulled away.

"This is me," she reminded him a little resentfully.

"You don't have to tell me. The beautiful younger sister. I know very well."

Lydia shrugged disbelievingly. But his face was two inches from hers and she knew that all her life had been leading up to this moment. She hadn't known it would happen in a chilly spring twilight in a rather dingy street two blocks from Waterloo railway station, nor with a man who a very short time since had been about to marry her sister, and who was still closing his eyes and believing that it was Aurora's lips he kissed. It should have been a long way from heaven, but actually heaven seemed very close indeed.

Philip lifted his head. "Are you hungry? Come back to my rooms. I'll light a fire and we'll have some wine. Let's get that taxi."

The cruising taxi stopped and Lydia climbed into its darkness. She found that she was trembling again. Dumb little fool! she apostrophised herself. You're only the younger sister. You happen to be the one who's here. But the trembling persisted, and when he put his arm round her shoulders she leaned against him, trying to grow calm, hoping he wouldn't notice her agitation.

How was it if one loved and the other didn't? Better, anyway, than the sorry affair of M'sieu Bertrand when there had been no love on either side. And the memory of the long, perplexing day was dying. There was only this cool darkness, and the solid form of the taxi-driver blocking the swinging lights in the streets from view, and the feel of Philip's hand over hers.

He had two rooms at the top of a tall house in Chelsea, one a bedroom and the other a large, rather bare studio. Lydia, in her haze of delight, found it wonderful and enchanting after the luxury of Greenhill. It occurred to her to wonder if Aurora had contrasted the two places, and decided that Philip's was the more likeable of the two.

But Aurora did not belong here tonight. Lydia walked about restlessly while Philip lit the fire. When he was in the tiny kitchen getting out a bottle of wine and glasses she looked at her face in the small circle of her compact mirror, and saw that her eyes were deeply green and shining. She combed her hair, smoothing it into glossiness. Would Philip care for this thin, pointed and eager face? Or would he close his eyes again and pretend that it was Aurora's, that the slim, taut body his remembering hands moved over was also Aurora's.

Or perhaps he would not touch her again. For he wouldn't know, unless her darkened eyes told him, that she longed to be touched.

"Is the fire burning?" he called.

"Yes. Beautifully."

"Why don't you sit down?"

"I don't want to."

"Then come out here and help me. Can you cook?"

Lydia stood in the minute kitchen watching him cut up a French loaf. "A little. Not *haute cuisine*."

"That's better than Aurora. Goodness knows what she lived on when she was alone. Cigarettes and China tea."

"Didn't you know her better than that?"

"No. Not in the simple ways. Such as how she brushed her hair or how she looked when she woke up in the mornings, or even how she felt when it was a fine sunny day."

"But you were going to find all those things out," Lydia murmured.

"Yes. Perhaps. Your eyes are green tonight."

"Are they?"

"Let's go by the fire. We can eat later."

"Philip, I'm not Aurora," she said again.

"No." His eyes were narrowed to a gleam. "But you're the girl who kept me waiting three hours. That's something, isn't it?"

"I won't be used like a drug to make you forget," she said angrily, waiting for him to come and kiss her.

"You're a drug all on your own, I assure you."

For a moment they faced each other.

"I mean it, Lydia," he said, in a roughened voice, but as at last he took her in his arms, at the precise moment when she almost believed in his urgency and sincerity, the telephone rang. The firelit silence was shattered. Lydia sprang away as if suddenly they were not alone.

106

"Damn!" Philip exclaimed, and picking up the receiver spoke curtly, "Hullo! Hullo!"

Then very slowly he said, "Aurora!" and stopped, as if he couldn't believe his ears.

Lydia wanted to weep. But her eyes were quite dry. This was not a pain to bring tears. It was too anguished for that.

Aurora! As if she had been watching them, waiting for the exact moment to break their dream. Or Lydia's dream, not Philip's. He had only been fooling himself, and almost successfully, too.

"Where are you? . . . Where do you want me to come? . . . I can't hear what you're saying. Yes! You're. . . . What's that? . . . Oh! It's a bit late for that, isn't it. . . . Yes, of course I'm all right, if such a small matter interests you." His voice had become off-hand and haughty. "What? . . . Yes, my darling, of course I wish you well. You wouldn't like to tell me where you are or who you're with? . . . I'm not inquisitive, but your mother and sister—— What's that? I can't hear! This is a bad line. Aurora! Are you there? Oh, for heaven's sake! We've been cut off."

He put the receiver down, and said without turning, "She's been cut off. There seemed to be a lot of interference. I haven't a clue where she was ringing from."

Lydia crushed down her private and very personal disappointment.

"What did she say?"

"I couldn't hear properly. First of all something about would I come and get her, things had gone wrong. And then she began to laugh and said she was fooling to see how I would react. Everything was splendid, but she was sorry she'd played such a dirty trick on me. She just wanted to tell me that. Then we were cut off."

"How did she sound?"

"Rather odd, actually. Almost as if she were a little drunk. Or half asleep."

Drunk! That would be possible, Lydia thought, remembering the secreted bottle of gin. But the other state of strange drowsiness brought back that fantasy of Aurora on her forgotten bed, hidden behind the climbing nettles and cob-webs. The sleeping princess awaiting rescue. . . .

"Philip, are you sure it was her?"

Now he turned and she saw that his face was narrowed and hard. "Quite sure."

"What can we do?"

"There is nothing to do, is there? She was only belatedly apologising for her behaviour."

"But those voices in the background."

"I told you it was a bad line. I think we'd got in on someone else's conversation. To tell the truth I'm not very interested in Aurora's tricks. Are you? Let's eat, shall we?"

He made a sudden apologetic movement, touching her hair briefly. His face was rueful. But Lydia knew that their moment had gone. Aurora was back. Her haunting beauty and the mystery that surrounded her was a far more devastating weapon than the momentary angry green fire in Lydia's eyes.

Over the meal which now neither of them wanted they waited for the telephone to ring again and for Aurora to finish her cut-off conversation. Philip had taken the gold pendant from his pocket and thrown it on the table. It lay between them, a barrier as effective as may have been the upthrusting nettles round Aurora's imaginary bed.

"You'd better ring Armand Villette in the morning and tell him we have this," he said. "Ask him if he's had any instructions from Aurora. He's sacked his new secretary, by the way."

"Do you think that's significant? She might have been a dead loss. New secretaries often are nowadays."

"Yes. And after Aurora, who at least was decorative if not efficient."

Lydia's honesty forced her to say what was worrying her. "Philip, do you think Aurora was perhaps really ringing for help?"

"To save her from the wrong man? I think she'll have to sort that out for herself." His voice was bitter and a little derisive, but even so Lydia sensed his uneasiness. Supposing Aurora were not just being provocative and changeable, crook-

108

ing her finger with superb confidence when she wanted to win back a discarded lover, but really were in some strange kind of danger, and had not been allowed to say so.

"I think I'll go home," she said wearily. "It's been a long day."

"I'll take you."

"No, just get me a taxi, please."

"I'll take you," he repeated.

"But the telephone might ring."

"That can't be helped, can it? Put your coat on."

He didn't attempt to touch her now. He sounded tired and impatient, and she herself felt she no longer cared what happened. If he made love to her she would passively submit, if he didn't it didn't matter. Too much emotion and weariness had made everything neutral, dull, melancholy.

13

The girl lying in the big bed opened her heavy eyes to see who was rousing her.

"So you don't trust me, darling! You don't love me after all!"

She could see the brilliance of his eyes, his faintly smiling mouth, the lines and hollows of his adored face. Pleasure stirred in her tired body. Her mind was in a curious blurred state, and did not at once remember everything.

"I do love you," she insisted. "I do."

"Then why did you try to run back to your artist?"

"Oh! You were told!"

"Of course I was told. What did you expect?" His fingertips touched her forehead, her cheeks. She was so sleepy and warm, it was delicious.

"Did you think he could make you happier than I could?"

"No, not happier. No." Her mind struggled with the blurred images. Something awoke, a tension, a feeling of terror. "But safer," she added, and then shrank back from the scorn in his eyes. Although he still smiled.

"Who wants safety? Wouldn't you find it a little dull? Especially without me?"

She wanted him to scoop her up and hold her tightly in his arms. At the same time she shrank from his touch for some obscure reason she couldn't quite remember. The conflicting emotions left her deadly tired.

"Yes," she said obediently, "I expect I would. Very dull."

"Then be a good girl." He bent to kiss her lightly. "Don't do that again."

His voice was too light and affectionate to hold a threat. But the threat was there. She knew that now. Beneath everything, the pleasure, the love-making, the comfort in which she lived, there was the threat. Sometimes it didn't bother her too much, she thought the compensations were sufficient, but at other times the icy terror swept over her and she wanted to call to anybody, even a passing stranger, for help.

But that was only when she was alone and tense with wakefulness, and the least stir in the house, even the calling of owls in the garden, filled her with apprehension. When she was full of this heavy drowsiness, as at this moment, nothing mattered. She had forgotten what it was she was afraid of, and wanted only to sleep.

14

Lydia had to ring three times in the morning before she got a reply from Armand Villette's office. Then, in response to his familiar, deep, rather irritable voice, "Hullo? Who is it?" she said, "It's Lydia Deering, Mr. Villette. I wondered how your aunt was settling down. I got fond of her, you know. I'm really interested."

"Oh, she's fine." Subtly, the brusque impatience of his voice changed to geniality. "She's written to you, I believe. She has this thing about letters, hasn't she? Wrote one to herself, too, and I had to post it in town. Well, it's a harmless eccentricity. I think you can decide she's in good hands now, Miss Deering. Her sister's delighted to have her down there. Bygones are bygones, and all that. So don't worry any more about it. I was about to ring you, as it happens. I've no secretary at the moment, and things are in rather a muddle."

"Why were you going to ring me?"

"Just to thank you for your very kind care of Aunt Clara, and to tell you you can put her out of your mind now. What are you going to do yourself, in the immediate future?"

"Oh, probably going back to Paris," Lydia, with some astonishment, heard herself saying. "I was working there when I had to come home for Aurora's wedding."

"That sounds most interesting. I wish you well." Did his voice sound relieved? She couldn't be sure. "By the way, I suppose you haven't heard from your sister again?"

She shut out of her mind that mocking, inopportune call to Philip last night, and said casually, "There was just her message about the pendant you gave her. I forgot to tell you yesterday. She asked me to return it to you for safe keeping. Did you know?"

"No. Certainly I didn't. In that case, perhaps you'd better drop it in to my office. I'll be here all day."

"Actually, I've decided to keep it myself until Aurora comes back for it herself," Lydia said. "I think she owes us—or Philip, anyway—that, at least. She's been too casual altogether."

There was a very brief silence. "But if you're going to Paris, Miss Deering——"

"Oh, I'll arrange with my mother or Philip to keep it."

"You wish to take the responsibility?"

"Oh, heavens, yes. It isn't really valuable."

Afterwards she realised that the pendant had been Armand Villette's wedding gift to Aurora and that she had not been very flattering about it. There were two other things she realised—that Armand Villette was happy to think she was leaving London, and that he would very much have liked to get the pendant into his possession.

Well, she would thwart him in both of those objects.

But why did it matter?

Truthfully she wished she were going away. Less than a week ago she had rushed home so happily, and what had happened? Aurora had disappeared and left Philip haunted by her, and she, Lydia in her turn, was fool enough to become haunted and obsessed by Philip.

It was not to be wondered at that she felt flat, tired and disillusioned. She began to think seriously of going back to Paris, not to the Bertrands but to some other, more pleasant, family. And if Philip decided he did care for her a little he could follow her.

Lydia sat in front of Aurora's mirror, her chin in her hands, gazing glumly at herself. The fleeting, green-eyed brilliance she had had last night had gone. Her eyes were no colour, her hair too straight, her cheeks vaguely hollowed. The glass that had so often held the exquisite oval of Aurora's face now held this white-cheeked urchin. Yet she had ambitiously hoped to impose this image, instead of Aurora's, in Philip's mind.

When the telephone rang she sprang up guiltily, afraid that the caller was Philip and that he would somehow be able to see as well as hear her melancholy.

It was Millicent, with her daily anxious enquiry as to whether there were any more news. Lydia listened gloomily to her high, expectant voice, and had to pull herself together to relate the news of Aurora's telephone call last evening.

Millicent listened in a silence punctuated by suppressed exclamations of disapproval.

Then she said, "I can't understand her, Lydia. She's being so tantalising. Like a cat playing with a mouse." (Except that Philip was no mouse, as Aurora had yet to discover.)

"Do you think someone is making her do this?"

"Who?" Lydia asked sharply.

"Darling, how should I know? But it's so unlike Aurora. She may be flighty, but she isn't cruel."

"She wasn't very cruel last night. She was apologising."

"That's all very well, but if she were truly sorry she would leave Philip alone. It must be just too galling for him. Don't you agree?"

"I expect so," Lydia said helplessly.

"Darling, what's the matter? You sound so glum. Why don't you come home? There's no point in staying in that horrid empty flat any longer."

"Yes, I know. I think I will come home."

She didn't want to stay even for another hour in the flat, yet something compelled her to. It couldn't have been the possibility of a telephone call from Philip, because she had nothing to say to him if he did ring. The flat was dreadfully empty and lonely. When June Birch asked her down to coffee she accepted almost eagerly.

But there wasn't much point to that either. June, with her molten-gold hair and inquisitive eyes, was a person one would normally want to avoid.

"You've been awfully quiet up there, duck. Nothing happening?"

"What's likely to happen now?"

"Oh, something will happen. We haven't heard the last of Aurora, not a dramatic person like that. She'll be back for her things, anyway, won't she? And to wind up her affairs." June laughed noisily. "That sounds a bit morbid, doesn't it? I mean to cancel the lease and so on."

"It's not Aurora you're expecting, is it?" Lydia said slowly. "It's the person with the key to her flat."

June nodded affably. "I don't mind telling you I'm breaking my neck to see that bird."

"He's the man she's married, of course."

"Maybe, but I don't believe a fly-by-night like that would get married. He'd be hard to catch. Well, of course, she might be just living with him, mightn't she? Take sugar in your coffee, duck? You're looking a bit peaky. What's wrong? Not sleeping?"

"I'm worried," Lydia confessed.

"Not falling for that good-looking artist, are you?"

"Of course I'm not!"

June looked at her shrewdly. "You're a nice kid, but no one forgets a person like Aurora overnight. Do they? Give him time."

How much time, Lydia wondered, as she returned upstairs. When the postman dropped a letter through the door she had a wild hope that it might be from Philip finishing what he had begun to say when Aurora's inopportune telephone call had come.

But it was only the one Armand had told her to expect from Miss Wilberforce. It was a short, stilted, bread-and-butter letter, and had in it none of the rambling charm Lydia would have expected.

"My dear Lydia,

"This is to thank you once again for your very great kindness to me, a stranger, and to tell you that I am extremely happy and contented here. My sister Blandina could not be more kind, though it is sad her health is so precarious. However, she is already a great deal better, and we are talking of a trip abroad quite soon. The weather is delightful, and my nephew Armand full of thoughtfulness for my comfort. So please do not feel you have to think any more about me or my small, unimportant affairs. I am an old woman and a stranger who does not wish to intrude on your life. I wish you every happiness and good fortune in the future, and so goodbye, my dear Lydia.

"Your grateful friend,

"Clara Wilberforce."

When Philip at last rang, Lydia's melancholy had given way to some ashamed tears. Even Miss Wilberforce did not need her any more, and was gently, gracefully, saying goodbye. Now she felt of use to nobody. She really would go back to Paris, perhaps even, in desperation, to the Bertrand family.

"What's the matter?" came his brisk voice.

"Nothing's the matter. Oh, well, yes, I'm rather sad because I've just had a letter from Miss Wilberforce. Saying goodbye."

"Really! That isn't like her, is it?"

"As a waif and stray, it isn't, but she's in the bosom of her family now. Even talking of trips abroad. It's a very nice

114

letter. I think she feels she shouldn't worry me any more. After all, I was a complete stranger."

"But a very nice one," said Philip with maddening kindness. "Even I thought so." Was he saying goodbye, too? Her heart sank still lower. "Well, it goes to prove what I said last night, doesn't it? We can wash our hands of this business, and say farewell to the whole lot of them, Miss Wilberforce and all."

"I suppose so."

"After all, no one's dead, no one's hurt, no one's in trouble."

"I know."

"Then what? Can I come round and see you?"

Not in that polite tone of voice, she thought.

"I'm just planning to catch a train home. Millicent wants me to come and there doesn't seem to be anything to do here. I've rung Armand and told him I'm keeping the pendant in the meantime, in case he gets any messages from Aurora. He seemed slightly disturbed about that, but I couldn't be sure. I'm beginning to read double meanings into everything. So I think a little while at home is a good idea. June can keep an eye on this flat. Or you can, if you like."

She realised she hadn't let him say anything for some time, and waited for him to speak.

"Would you like me to come down with you?"

"Good heavens, no! I imagine you never want to see that place again."

"I'll come if you want me to."

"No. I said no."

"Very definite, aren't you? Then what train are you catching? I'll see you off."

"There's no need even to do that," she said tightly.

"Lydia darling, you sound as if you hate me all at once. You think that I, like Aurora, was only fooling last night."

"Of course I do," she said lightly. "So was I. All right, then, come to Waterloo if you insist. I'll catch the four forty-five."

But that was a mistake, too. Her taxi got into a traffic jam and she arrived with only a minute or two to spare. She hadn't even time to assess the look on his face, whether it was anxiety that she would miss her train or pain that she was going.

115

"Damn it, Lydia, now I haven't time to say a thing."

She laughed. "Goodbye, Philip. Take care of yourself. What are you going to do now?"

"Oh, carry on with that exhibition. It's supposed to open next week. Can I send you an invitation?"

"I'd love one, thank you. I hope it's a tremendous success."

"Lydia, don't do anything more about that old woman or anyone without letting me know."

"I don't intend to do anything more at all. It's over as far as I'm concerned. I must fly."

But he had bought a platform ticket and was following her. The train was about to move. A porter was slamming doors. Philip wrenched one open and helped Lydia in.

"Shall I come with you?"

She laughed again, although momentarily her heart had leaped. He had sounded eager.

"Don't be an idiot. You've got more important things to do."

"Lydia, I hurt you last night, didn't I? I didn't mean to. . . ." But now the train was moving, and when at last he had begun to say important things she could no longer hear them.

She could only stand and wave and smile until his tall form was indiscernible, and he himself would not be able to see the tears run down her cheeks.

Lipham was unbelievably the same as it had been a week ago. The swans still floated on the dark, weedy pond, the trees hung heavily over pools of shadow, even the flowers in the garden looked the same, as if no petals had fallen.

Millicent greeted Lydia warmly, but warned her not to talk about Aurora to Geoffrey as he was very touchy indeed about her. They were just behaving as if nothing had happened, as if Aurora were in London doing a job, and had never come home to be married.

Or as if she no longer existed, Lydia thought privately. As if she were dead.

It was when she went into Aurora's bedroom and saw in the wardrobe her belongings, the unworn wedding-dress, and the

116

honeymoon clothes, that it seemed as if Aurora really had died.

She shut the door hastily, and decided that her father after all was the wisest for putting the matter out of his mind. She would try to do the same.

There was only one small matter to wind up in connection with the confused events of the week, and that was to answer Miss Wilberforce's letter. For, in spite of Miss Wilberforce's courteous but firm goodbye, she remembered the old lady's passion for receiving letters.

She would like to have written, "Don't let Blandina put it across you. She isn't as ill as she pretends to be." The firm hand drawing the curtains that evening had not been that of a very sick woman. But that was none of her business, and the main thing was Miss Wilberforce's contentment.

After all, what would they have done with her had nephew Armand not turned up?

Last of all, that night, Lydia thought of Philip and the sentence the moving train had cut off. What had it been going to be? An apology? A declaration of sincerity?

She didn't know. She wished she could put him out of her mind also.

But none of them were really out of her mind, Philip, Aurora, Miss Wilberforce, Blandina, Armand Villette, even the gardener with his intent, stony gaze jostled in her dreams that night. She had, she knew obscurely, finished with none of them.

Two days later, when Miss Wilberforce's answer to her letter arrived, she was appalled by her stupidity and complacency. How could she have believed, in face of what she had seen, that all was well? Blandina had not assumed her illness for her sister, but for Lydia, to pull the wool over Lydia's eyes. As soon as Lydia had gone she had risen, strong and well, to assume command of the household, to bully her gentle, nervous sister, to keep out intruders. . . .

But all that Lydia had pushed out of her mind, because she had been thinking of nothing but Philip and her unhappiness about him. She had been selfish and cowardly and deliberately stupid. Now something must be done.

In the same post as Miss Wilberforce's letter there was an invitation to Philip's exhibition. It had written across it, "Please do come."

It was an appropriate excuse to return to London. All at once she did not know how she could have stayed away.

15

It was the second time that Miss Wilberforce had heard steps in the night. She cunningly lay very still, pretending to be asleep, while the steps came nearer, halting beside her bed. A shaft of light through the half-open door showed her the woman's form, the arm which reached out and deftly removed the glass of lemon and barley water from her bedside table, substituting another glass.

The woman was very thin and wore some dark garment. Both times she had come it had not been possible to see her face. She had been quick and silent, sliding away as softly as she had come. Miss Wilberforce had been too nervous and agitated to sit up and cry out.

The next time, she told herself, licking dry lips, she would do something. She would say, "Who is that? Is it Blandina?"

But she was certain it was not Blandina.

Besides, why would Blandina be prowling about in the night changing glasses of cordial? She wasn't well enough to do such things, and she wasn't so secretive. For what had been wrong with the cordial in the previous glass, or, more important, what was wrong with this one?

Yes, that was the point. The action of the night-time prowler was highly suspicious, and Miss Wilberforce was not going to be tricked into drinking the new liquid. As soon as she thought it was safe, and indeed as soon as her trembling legs would obey her, she got out of bed and took the glass to the washbasin and emptied it.

That would foil them, she thought with satisfaction.

All the same, she still felt ill, as she had done for several days. She knew she would not sleep again, so leaving the light on she sat up in bed with her large black handbag propped beside her and tried to absorb herself in the familiar pleasure of re-reading her correspondence. There were the letters that had come yesterday, the one from that charming girl, Lydia, who wrote so sweetly about keeping in touch, and letting her know if ever she were in trouble again, and the one she had written to herself which Armand had kindly posted for her in London so that it really looked as if she had had an exciting trip to town.

That contained no real news, of course, but it was comforting to read it, because it made Greenhill seem such a pleasant place.

"The birds sing and the May trees are in flower. The gardener keeps the gardens very nicely, though he does spend too much time near the house, and is inclined to neglect the lawns and beds farther away. I think he gets a little lonely, and likes to be within reach of voices. My nephew Armand does not come home every night as the journey is too arduous after a busy day. My sister Blandina, considering her poor health, and also that she has only been here a month, runs the house with admirable efficiency. I have been very poorly ever since the day after my arrival, and have had to keep to my room. But I am getting much better, with all this wonderful care. . . ."

Miss Wilberforce smiled with gentle pleasure as she read this letter. She really did seem to be having a nice time in the country. The birds singing, the flowers blooming, the care she received when she was ill. This latter trouble she attributed to the unaccustomed rich food which was very different from the bread and cheese and boiled egg diet she had been living on in London.

She sat up in bed, her white hair mussed, her scrawny neck poking out of her silk nightgown (one of Blandina's, Blandina had always liked good things), her apple cheeks a little faded and blanched as if the country air, oddly enough, did not suit her, her fragile hands searching busily in the fat black bag.

119

What was this? Oh, yes, Lydia's letter from Lipham, full of kind concern. She would answer that presently, although Blandina had said that Lydia would not want to be bothered any more with a perfect stranger, and she must bring that friendship to an end.

But it was not true that Lydia did not want to be bothered any more, for this letter expressly asked her to write if she were in any trouble.

Was she in trouble, apart from feeling ill, and having that strange woman messing about with her drinking glass at nights, and apart from Blandina being rather more bossy than one remembered her, and also bewilderingly changed in appearance?

No, she wasn't in trouble exactly. But planning what she might write to Lydia was comforting, as also was re-reading her letters.

She scrabbled in the bag again, and brought out another folded sheet of paper. What was this letter? It looked rather new, as if she had not read it very often. The handwriting was strange. There was no address at the top, nor indeed any signature, and it contained only a couple of lines. But it was for her, undoubtedly. It read,

"Dear Miss Wilberforce,
"Don't stay here. They are all murderers. Go back to London and get a pension. You'll be far better off."

Miss Wilberforce gave a gasp, and dropped the paper as if it had been a beetle. Good gracious, how had *that* got into her bag? It hadn't come in the post, surely. She didn't remember having seen it before.

But she must have done, because here it was, removed from its envelope (and of course all letters were originally in envelopes with stamps), and put carefully in her bag.

How very odd! She just didn't remember having seen it before. And what a horrid letter it was. So vindictive!

As if Blandina and that kind middle-aged nephew of hers, Armand Villette, were murderers! Blandina had always been

120

overbearing and unreasonable, it was true, and she was even more so in her old age, but she had never committed a murder, one was sure of that. And as for Armand, he was so fumbling, and rather shy and kind, he wouldn't hurt a soul.

Really, what a nasty, mischief-making letter for anyone to write. She would stuff it right to the bottom of her bag where she wouldn't come across it again for a long time. She would keep all the pleasant ones on top.

Murderers! How absurd!

Though one did have those uneasy feelings about Blandina looking so unlike herself. That was, if one remembered accurately how she had used to look. But surely one didn't remember that very long nose, or the sharpness of her eyes. Age was to blame for those changes of feature, of course. Poor thing, she couldn't help it if her bossiness had come out, at last, in her nose. And she was very brave about not giving in to illness. She had determined to improve from the moment Miss Wilberforce arrived. And she talked at great length about things they had done as children, particularly their visits to the seaside at Bournemouth, and old Nanny, and one or two other people whom Miss Wilberforce had completely forgotten.

All the same, marriage to the long-deceased Mr. Paxton must have changed her a great deal. Sometimes she sounded like a complete stranger.

And there was this annoying way she had of telling Miss Wilberforce what she must write in her letters, especially to Lydia. One hadn't been able to tell Lydia any real news in that first letter. Blandina had stood over her saying, "Your wits are a little feeble, Clara. You can't write that rambling nonsense. Just say this. . . ."

And she had slowly and clearly dictated what must be written, while Miss Wilberforce's shaky hand followed behind, unwillingly but helplessly.

"There," she had said, "that's a very satisfactory, courteous letter, and now you mustn't bother that girl with your affairs any more. It simply isn't done, Clara. It's the height of thoughtlessness and selfishness."

But why not now, Miss Wilberforce thought excitedly, in the silence of this very early morning, write to Lydia exactly as she wanted to. Then, as soon as it was daylight, she could dress and go for a delightful early morning stroll into the village to post the letter. That way, Blandina need know nothing at all about it. She would be back in her room for breakfast without anyone being aware that she had gone out. She was sure she was strong enough, after all this resting in her room, to take a walk. It would do her good.

Excitement brought a little colour into her cheeks. Miss Wilberforce pattered about the room getting out notepaper and pen and ink, and climbing back into bed with them began happily to write.

She wouldn't tell about that silent figure changing the glass on her bedside table in the night, for that might alarm Lydia into thinking she was being poisoned, when of course she was much too shrewd for that. Nor would she mention the strange letter that had somehow, by mistake, got into her handbag. But she would express her doubts and vague fear of her sister Blandina.

"She has changed so remarkably, Lydia. Of course I know I haven't seen her for very many years, and age does strange things to one. Marriage, perhaps, too, to that Mr. Paxton whom she never mentions, so probably he was not a good husband. And I know she always despised me because she thought I was silly and empty-headed. But I didn't think she would have grown old quite like this. Neither of our parents had *quite* such a prominent nose. . . ."

It was a wonderful relief to put all her strange doubts on paper. It made them seem foolish, and she began to wonder if she had invented them because, secretly, she was missing the busy, virile streets of London which she had adored.

When the letter was finished at last, scrawled over four sheets of paper, it was growing daylight, and the first birds were singing.

Now for the daring part of her plan, to get up and dress and slip out of the house to walk to the village. Was she strong enough? Would her stomach, which had been so un-

122

reliable lately, misbehave again, or would she have one of those nasty dizzy turns?

No, she decided with relief. She felt better this morning. A little light in the head, because she had eaten so little lately, but otherwise quite well. She was sure she could manage the walk successfully, and be back in time for breakfast at eight o'clock.

Before she was dressed, however, all the birds were singing, and there was a distant clattering of dishes downstairs. Then she began to get fussed. Time was slipping by, and her clothes wouldn't seem to go on properly. Her hands trembled and she dropped a shoe with a clatter. But at last she was ready.

Then she discovered that although she had addressed the envelope to Lydia she had not put a stamp on it. It would be too early for the post office to be open. She must find a stamp in her bag. She knew she had one, or even two, but where were they? She had to turn out every mortal thing to find those two elusive scraps of paper, and when at last she had run them to earth in a fold of the lining she was hot and trembling. Precious time had gone by. It was nearly seven o'clock. She would have to hurry.

It was possible to descend the stairs without being observed. But crossing the hall too hastily her foolish old feet tripped in a rug, and as she stumbled Jules, the gardener, suddenly appeared behind her.

She didn't know which room he had come from. She was surprised to see him in this part of the house at all. Her surprise took away what little composure she had left, and she looked at him guiltily.

"Good morning, Jules."

"Good morning, madam. You're not going out?"

He was a tall, slim, very straight person, with a peculiar arrogance, considering his position in life. He must have been very spoilt. Armand, no doubt, had been much too easy with him, and Blandina had always been foolish about good-looking men.

"Yes, I am," she managed to say in reply to his shocked question. "It's such a beautiful morning, and I was awake

123

early. I thought I'd take a little stroll. I haven't been very well, you know."

"I'm sorry, madam. Then should you walk far?"

Did he need to speak so loud? In a moment those sharp ears of Blandina's would hear and she would come pouncing out of her room, like a great, long-nosed cat.

"You weren't planning to go all the way to the village with that letter, madam?"

His eyes were on the letter which, idiot old creature that she was, she had failed to conceal. But goodness me, why should a gardener, even a spoilt and arrogant one, interfere with her plans?

She gave her untidy white head a toss, refusing haughtily to make explanations.

"I am merely going for a stroll, Jules. Good morning."

But it was too late. Blandina had heard. She was at the head of the stairs calling in her loud, imperative voice, "Clara, whatever are you doing out of bed at this hour? Are you mad?"

Miss Wilberforce felt as if she were crumpling inside. Indeed, her legs literally were crumpling, and she had to grope for one of the tall-backed chairs and sit down.

"I was only going to post my letter," she said, with the sudden petulance of an old woman. "I don't see why I shouldn't be allowed to post it in the village if it gives me pleasure."

Jules, having caused the mischief, had discreetly disappeared, and Blandina was coming down the stairs. Clad in a dark red, wool dressing-gown, with her iron-grey hair scraped back from her bony forehead, and her black eyes glittering, she looked ridiculously frightening. Ridiculously so, considering she was one's own sister.

"My dear Clara, you shall go to the village as often as you wish at a reasonable time of day, and when you are better. But tell me honestly, do you feel fit at this minute to walk a mile?"

Miss Wilberforce reluctantly shook her head. She had felt fit when she had got up. But now, after all this distress, she knew

124

she could not even have reached the end of the drive. It was doubtful if she could climb the stairs to her room.

"I'm sorry, Blandina. I suppose I was being foolish. But I so enjoy letters. You know I do. It isn't nearly so much fun if someone else posts them. Besides, you don't care for me to write to Lydia."

"So that's who you've been writing to. What have you said to her?"

Miss Wilberforce held the letter tightly, ready to tear it up if Blandina, in her overbearing way, demanded to see it.

"Nothing in particular. Just this and that. Lydia wrote to me, as you know, and it is only polite to answer."

"Of course," Blandina agreed, with unexpected amiability. "You don't have to tell me what is good manners. But I've told you before I don't want that nice child worried. She has no responsibility for you, and you simply can't intrude on her like this, Clara."

"Worried!" repeated Miss Wilberforce in pained surprise.

"Haven't you told her you've been ill?"

"Oh, in passing, yes. I didn't dwell on it."

"I think it's better not to mention it at all. You must listen to me, Clara. Armand and I are responsible for you now, and we know what's best. Now supposing you destroy that long, foolish, rambling letter you've got there—oh, yes, I know that's exactly what it is—and we'll go upstairs and remember our manners and write a polite, graceful note, as we did before. Isn't that the best idea? Of course it is."

Blandina was being kind! The unexpectedness of this, when she had expected sharp words and disfavour, filled Miss Wilberforce with remorse. Was she behaving very ungratefully?

And of course Blandina was right. One couldn't go on worrying Lydia, tempting as it was to spread one's thoughts all over a sheet of paper. No, one must behave with thoughtfulness and discretion.

Slowly Miss Wilberforce tore the letter in her hand into small pieces. She had temporarily forgotten the creeping figure in the night, doing strange things with her glass of

125

lemon and barley water, and the overbearing interfering way Blandina had. She was only conscious that now, for a little while at least, Blandina was being kind, and she was tremendously grateful. Besides she was beginning to feel ill and weak again. It would be nice to undress and get back into bed. No one made her get up if she didn't wish to. She could lie in the comfortable bed all day, watching the shadows move over the garden. The more ill she felt the less she longed to be back in London, holding her own with the jostling hurrying walkers down the hot pavements, window-shopping without resentment about her lack of money, listening to the virile cries of the paper boys, taking a sniff of the carnations on the corner stall, sharing a park bench with whoever else happened to be resting tired feet, buying her modest provisions for supper, and making her weary, cheerful way home. . . .

"Well, come then," Blandina was saying in her sharp way. "I'll help you upstairs. We'll write that letter after breakfast and Jules can take it to the post. Good gracious, you are shaky, aren't you? What will Doctor Neave say if he hears about this? You'd better spend the whole day in bed. Armand will be home tonight and you don't want him to see you looking so ill, do you?"

"I don't seem to recover as quickly as you did," Miss Wilberforce said meekly.

"Oh, mine was only one of my attacks. I told you that. They're only temporary. Different from your trouble, my poor Clara."

16

Lydia wandered about the gallery, vaguely unhappy that she could not at this moment concentrate on the pictures. They were full of colour and life, and she was pleased to hear murmurs of appreciation from the small crowd which had come to the opening of Philip's exhibition. She was remorseful that she had not previously had the time or opportunity to see Philip's work. It had never been that she was not interested, but other matters had got in the way.

Since honesty was one of her less comfortable virtues, she had also to admit to herself that jealousy had come into it. It was as a painter that Philip had first been interested in Aurora, and to Lydia Aurora was now associated inextricably with his work. Even here, in these luxuriant tropical canvases, she seemed to see Aurora's radiant white skin behind the brown-bodied native girls, as if even then she had been his exact dream, awaiting fulfilment.

"Lydia!" Philip had escaped from the small knot of people surrounding him, and was at her side. He had been going to say he was pleased she had come. That was clear enough because he had that polite look on his face. But as he looked down at her he said no more at all, merely gave her his disconcerting blue stare which told her nothing.

"Philip, I think your pictures are wonderful. I should have seen them before."

He raised an eyebrow. "We haven't had much time, have we? You were only in my studio once, and then——" He didn't mention Aurora's name, but went on quickly, "You didn't write to me. I suppose there's been no news?"

"Only a letter from Miss Wilberforce that seems rather alarming. I can't show it to you now. Later——"

There were people crowding round with congratulatory smiles. They were all strangers. They looked on Philip as a brilliant young artist, tremendously lucky to be holding a successful exhibition in London. They didn't know him as a jilted bridegroom burying his beautiful and unattainable dream.

Philip took Lydia's arm. "Hang around. I'll slip away at four o'clock. There's a coffee bar round the corner. I'll see you there."

An hour later, in this cosy gloom, redolent of coffee and expensive pastries, Lydia produced the letter which had given her an almost sleepless night, and watched Philip read it.

It wasn't fair to do this to him in the middle of his exhibition, but once more events seemed to be concerned with life and death.

Lydia knew the letter off by heart.

"Dear Lydia,

"Thank you for your letter. It gave me great pleasure. But as I have already said, there is no need to worry about me, as I have my future very well taken care of. I cannot impose on your time and kindness any more. But I wish you happiness and good fortune wherever you may be.
"Your friend,
"Clara Wilberforce."

That was fine. That was on the lines of the previous letter, a second reminder dictated obviously by another person that now she must keep out of Miss Wilberforce's life.

But the postcript had not been dictated by anybody. It had been scrawled across the bottom in large jerky writing:

I'm ill. I need help. Please come.

Philip looked up. "What do you think?"

"Why, that the postscript is the only part of the letter that's genuine."

"It's not the same handwriting."

"Don't you think so? Don't you think that could be the way Miss Wilberforce wrote when she was in a great hurry and very distressed? Or even drugged. Because of her illness, of course."

"Could be." Philip turned the envelope over. "This has been opened and sealed down again."

"I know. I noticed that at once."

"Hardly the work of a person who's dopey with drugs."

"No, but Miss Wilberforce isn't completely dumb. If Blandina has been too interfering she'd find a way of getting her own back. Blandina has said I'm not to come, and Clara wants me. That's how I see it. How ever she managed to send this message, she did send it." Lydia raised her eyes to his. "So I have to go."

"Of course you have to, Lydia dear. It's not your business, and I'm pretty certain you're not going to be very welcome to either Blandina or her devious nephew Armand, whatever

128

their game may be. But you can't resist a *cri de coeur*. Neither of us can. We'll have to go."

"We!"

His level eyes met hers.

"Did you think I'd let you go alone this time? Not on your life. I've wanted an excuse to see the respectable Armand's hideout, anyway. Now look. I can leave things here to my agent in another hour or so. I'll just make the polite farewells. Have you any idea what time trains leave for this place?"

"Not very often. Let's ring up and ask."

"No, I've a better idea. I'll borrow or hire a car." He sprang up. "Let's say in an hour from outside here. What are you going to do now?"

"Drink coffee," said Lydia dreamily. "Think of what we're going to say to Blandina. Poor, sweet old Clara. We're too fond of her not to pay her a visit occasionally, aren't we? We were just passing through the village. . . ."

Philip drove up to the front door with a flourish. It was late dusk, but the curtains, Lydia noticed, were not drawn. She remembered Blandina's tall, sombre form from her last visit, appearing theatrically to sweep them across, and all at once her heart was beating uncomfortably.

"Come along," said Philip, opening the car door. He looked at her again. "You're not nervous, surely?"

"I am. Madly."

"Idiot. What can happen? This is a social call. Let's hope Armand is home. Besides, I'm here."

He grinned at her comfortably, and suddenly she was extra-ordinarily happy.

"Remember, we don't mention Clara's letter," she said. "We've just called to see how she is."

They could hear the distant ringing of the bell. It was some time before footsteps approached and the door was opened. There were no lights on, strangely enough, and it was framed against darkness that Lydia recognised Jules, the gardener.

He was dressed in an open shirt and corduroy trousers. If he were acting as butler his attire was very casual. But one would never produce servility in that arrogant head or cold blue gaze.

"Madam!" he exclaimed in surprise, recognising Lydia.

"How do you do, Jules?" she said affably. "Is Miss Wilberforce in? We're giving her a surprise."

His eyes flicked from one to the other of them. He threw the door wide open, hospitably.

"Will you come in, please. Mr. Villette isn't home, but I'll let Mrs. Paxton know you're here."

They were taken into the spacious, well-furnished hall, and lights were switched on.

"I don't think she's very well, madam. But just wait, will you?"

Jules, with his long, athletic stride, disappeared.

Lydia looked at Philip. "Cloakroom through that door," she said reminiscently. "I only saw this place clearly when I arrived the other day. After that I was plastered. Nice, isn't it?"

Philip looked round with interest. "One would hardly have expected such good taste from Armand. A scruffy little man like that."

"Yes, I know. Perhaps all those dead and gone aunts are responsible. One can imagine Aunt Blandina——"

Although her voice had been low, Lydia could not repress a guilty start when, from the stairway, Aunt Blandina's dramatic voice answered her.

"Miss Deering! What a surprise! But you should have let us know you were coming."

She was descending the stairs, leaning slightly on a stick. She wore a long, dark-coloured gown, and looked immensely tall. Her hair, scraped back severely from her bony yellow forehead, made her face, with its strong jutting nose and intense eyes, look like a painting of some medieval martyr. There was no softness there. Even her polite smile was a facial contortion only. She was deep in her unhumorous, severe world. Though she leaned on her stick it was not possible that she needed it. Her body was full of tough, ancient strength.

Only the bedclothes and the soft pillows had hidden it and deceived Lydia when last she had seen her.

130

"How do you do, Mrs. Paxton?" Lydia said easily. If Blandina's apparent strength concealed weakness, so did her own calm voice conceal a suddenly racing heart. "This is a friend of mine, Philip Nash. We were passing this way on our way to the coast and thought—at least, it was my idea—that we'd like to call on Miss Wilberforce. I hope she's feeling better."

The brilliant black eyes of the old lady stabbed her. "You knew she was ill?"

"Jules has just told us. We're so sorry. Can we see her? She knows Philip. He met her at my flat."

"She's not at all well," Blandina said repressively. "In fact, I called the doctor again today. The trouble is partly nervous, as I guessed. Clara always had a weak stomach. I remember as children—but I won't go into those distressing details, ruined parties and so on." She stopped to measure them with her disturbing eyes. "It was very kind of you to call in. Will you take some sherry with me?"

Only sherry, thought Lydia. Blandina hadn't nephew Armand's dash. She did not go in for mixing quick-action martinis.

"Mrs. Paxton, we *do* want to see Miss Wilberforce. She isn't too ill, is she? I mean, if she is," she added ingenuously, "the doctor would have sent her to hospital, wouldn't he?"

"We'll stay five minutes, no more," Philip promised.

The sharp eyes darted from one to the other. The reluctance was obvious—but was it reluctance which genuinely protected her sister's well-being?

"Wait here," she said at last. "I'll go up and see if Clara feels she could see a visitor. She found the doctor's visit rather trying."

"Thank you, Mrs. Paxton," Lydia said. "That is good of you. You're quite recovered yourself?"

Now it seemed as if the old woman were angrily trying to read Lydia's clear eyes.

"I'm not at all well," she said huffily. "You saw the other day how I am in one of my attacks. They can come on me at any moment. Do please sit down. Jules will bring you some

131

sherry. We have the greatest trouble in keeping servants, you know. The place is too isolated. They might have to exert themselves to get to a cinema, poor things. So Jules very kindly helps indoors as well."

"Oh," said Lydia politely. Armand, too, had made an explanation about servants and the village postmistress had said they came from London. It was very likely they wouldn't care about being in this quiet place.

There was no opportunity to talk with Philip, for as soon as Blandina had gone up the stairs in her slow, stately way Jules came with the sherry. He served them silently, his supercilious eyes looking at a point beyond their heads, yet observing, Lydia was sure, every slightest expression or movement they made.

The house was very quiet. She looked up the wide stairs and had a sudden crazy desire to run up them and along the passage at the top, throwing open all the closed doors. She imagined finding the ten bedrooms of which Armand had boasted, all occupied by old women, slowly mummifying. An army of ancient aunts, kept alive long after they should have died. And Armand himself, a strange nephew Bluebeard. . . .

Suddenly she shivered and didn't want to throw open any doors at all. She wondered for a moment why they had come, why they should think it was their duty to do something which Aurora had shirked doing about an old woman.

Then, as Jules went silently away, Blandina returned, descending the stairs as slowly as she had climbed them.

"You can go up for a little while. Just ten minutes. Clara wants to see you, of course, although she is very tired and shouldn't be getting excited. No, just you, Miss Deering," she added in her autocratic way, as both Philip and Lydia sprang up. "If you don't mind, Mr. Nash. One visitor is plenty, and my sister seems to have formed an attachment for Miss Deering." She spoke as if poor, silly Clara had always formed rash and impulsive friendships which had to be tactfully but firmly ended.

Lydia looked at Philip. He was ready to defy the rules of courtesy in someone else's house and come if she wished him

132

to. But that was perhaps going too far. After all, her own eyes would tell her how it was with Miss Wilberforce.

"Then wait for me, Philip," she said lightly. "I won't stay long."

Miss Wilberforce was sitting up in bed, the fragile pink of excitement in her cheeks. Her hair was soft and wild round her sunken face. All her robust sprightliness had left her, and she looked very frail indeed. She had failed rather distressingly since Lydia had last seen her.

"My dear child, how sweet of you to come!" she cried with pleasure. "What a lovely surprise for me!"

Lydia bent to kiss her. "I'm so sorry you're not well, Miss Wilberforce."

"Yes, isn't it too aggravating! All this beautiful country air and I can't be outdoors. I can't even walk to the post office."

The door opened slightly wider and there was Blandina's tall silent form. Lydia didn't know Blandina had followed her up the stairs. She wished she had been allowed to talk to Miss Wilberforce alone, but one couldn't order one's hostess out of the room.

Miss Wilberforce was annoyed, too, for a quick, almost furtive expression crossed her face. She licked her lips, and with great presence of mind finished her sentence.

"Not that I need to walk to the post office, for Blandina sees that my letters are posted. How are you, Lydia dear? What have you been doing?"

"Just staying with my parents. Doing nothing, really."

"And that nice young man?"

"Philip? He's downstairs."

"Here! But he must come up."

Blandina interposed firmly, "I think not, Clara. You're getting over-excited already. You know the doctor prescribed complete rest."

Miss Wilberforce sank back in the bed. She looked small and withered.

"Yes. I've had this upset. I ate some mushrooms one day and they didn't agree with me. I can't seem to throw off this

133

silly weakness. Blandina remembers I was always easily upset. She's been so kind. So patient."

The room was comfortable, even luxurious. Miss Wilberforce, in an expensive nightdress and woolly bedjacket, looked as if she were receiving all the petting and pampering Armand had promised. The doctor had been this afternoon. He obviously had not been unduly alarmed.

Yet she couldn't forget that scrawled line at the bottom of the letter, "*I need help. . . .*"

If only Blandina would leave her alone with Miss Wilberforce for five minutes! But it was clear she did not mean to do any such thing.

There was nothing for it but to say, "Then you're going to be all right, Miss Wilberforce? Can I help you in any way?"

"Help!" said Miss Wilberforce in surprise.

"Help!" repeated Blandina tartly. "Why, if I may ask, do you think my sister needs your help, Miss Deering?"

Lydia refused to be browbeaten.

"I know she doesn't seem to, but I hope she wouldn't hesitate to ask if she did. I imagine, if she doesn't soon improve, you'll send her to hospital or get her a good nurse."

Blandina's brilliant black eyes were narrowed and furious.

"After all, you haven't been well yourself, Mrs. Paxton," Lydia went on blandly. "And you say you can't get servants. You can't possibly do this kind of nursing yourself."

"Oh, but I'm going to be all right, Lydia," Miss Wilberforce said cheerfully. "It's sweet of you to worry, but really I will be all right."

"Of course you will be. But I'm going to keep in close touch all the same. So is Philip. We'll be popping in again, just any time."

"Oh, how nice, Lydia dear! What nice surprises you give me, bless you."

Lydia turned to go, her head in the air, defying the tall, possessive, angry old woman in the doorway. But suddenly she looked back.

"Have you any letters you'd like posted now, Miss Wilberforce? Philip and I can take them."

"My sister hasn't been well enough to write letters recently," Blandina put in in a tightly controlled voice.

Miss Wilberforce made an eager movement, instantly suppressed.

She merely said tiredly, "No, I don't think I have, dear. Or did I write one this morning? My memory's getting so bad. Look in my bag. Over there, on the dresser."

Was it a signal? Was the old lady shrewd enough to give her a signal, or was she really too cloudy and vague in her mind? Lydia took a risk. She opened the bulging bag and with a clumsy movement spilled its contents on the floor.

"Oh, dear!" she exclaimed. "I'm so sorry. I'll pick all these up. They all seemed to be addressed to you, Miss Wilberforce. Well, never mind, write to me as soon as you're well enough. I expect to hear how you are progressing, mind."

She was wearing a light loose coat with large pockets. It was easy enough, in her swift gathering up of the spilt letters, to thrust several of them into her pocket, especially the one that had borne strange handwriting that could, from the brief knowledge of it, be Aurora's. She hadn't expected her haphazard impulse to yield such a dividend.

Downstairs Philip was strolling about restlessly, and in the background Jules was busy with the tray of drinks.

"We must go now," Lydia said politely to Blandina. "We've a long way to drive. Are you ready, Philip? What a pity Mr. Villette isn't home. Do give him our regards, won't you?"

"Of course," said Blandina. She added, "Armand is not often home during the week. He finds it too far and prefers to stay at his club."

"How is Miss Wilberforce?" Philip asked Lydia.

"I thought she'd failed a great deal." Lydia met Blandina's hostile eyes. "Don't you think so, Mrs. Paxton?"

"She has scarcely eaten for a week. What can you expect? But she's a great deal better today. And kind as you are, Miss Deering, you mustn't think this is your responsibility."

"Oh, but we're so fond of her. Aren't we, Philip? We intend to call again in a day or two."

"Perhaps on our way back to London," Philip suggested.

"Yes, we'll certainly do that. If we're not a trouble, Mrs. Paxton."

Lydia smiled sweetly. In the background Jules suddenly rattled glasses as he picked up the tray. Blandina made a movement forward, leaning heavily on her stick.

"By all means do that, Miss Deering. But as soon as Clara recovers we mean to take that delayed holiday abroad. I would be gone by now if it hadn't been for Clara arriving like this. However, I don't expect we'll be able to leave for a day or two yet. So we shall probably be here when next you're kind enough to call."

She didn't hold out her hand. She merely waited for them to go. But just as Lydia turned to the door, feeling obscurely that she had failed, that there should be some social law giving an outsider the right to interfere between two sisters in one of the sister's homes, the doorbell rang.

The sound seemed to startle Blandina as much as it did Lydia. For a moment she stood rigid.

Then she said, "Jules!" and the tall man in the casual clothes crossed over to open the door.

Armand stood on the doorstep. The little, middle-aged, rather plump and shabby man, so out of place in this tasteful house, who did not come home during the week because of the distance, stood there silently disproving all his aunt had said.

He was as surprised to see them as they were him. He came forward with a quick, bustling movement, holding out his hand, exclaiming in a too loud voice, "Well, what a pleasant surprise! Miss Deering! Mr. Nash! I saw the car outside and thought it was the doctor's. Aunt Blandina, have you looked after these two young people? Have they been up to see poor Aunt Clara? She's not at all well, poor dear, but imagine if she were ill and still in that horrid bed-sitting-room!"

"We're just leaving," said Lydia pleasantly. "We've been promising to call again."

"Of course, of course. How kind! And tell me, has there been any news of your sister? My eloping secretary," he turned to explain to Blandina. His large, round eyes were rolling be-

136

hind their spectacles. They had their coy, jovial look. But his plump hands were clasped tightly together as if he were cold.

"Yes. We've heard from her," Philip answered briefly. "We know where she is, and hope to be having her back in London soon."

"Ah, indeed! With or without the dashing young husband, may I ask? But of course it will be with him. Inseparable, I imagine. You haven't decided to leave that gold pendant with me, as she asked, Miss Deering? Or do you still wish to take the responsibility?"

"Miss Deering is a young lady who enjoys responsibility," came Blandina's harsh voice. "Armand, we mustn't keep our guests standing here. They want to be on their way."

"Of course, of course. I've taken this unexpected trip down to see Aunt Clara. I've been worried about her. Then goodbye, Miss Deering, Mr. Nash. Do call again."

His affable voice followed them out into the night. It was a warm, early summer dusk, and perspiration glinted faintly on Armand's forehead. But he still gripped his hands together as if he were cold.

17

In the car, driving slowly towards the village, Lydia began to tick off points on her fingers.

"We were decidedly not welcome. In fact, we were very embarrassing callers. You were not encouraged to go up and see Clara, and I was not left alone with her. Why? Because she would tell me something I mustn't know? Blandina isn't, and never has been, I imagine, really ill. Then why did she pretend the other day, and how, in her present state of health and intelligence, could she have forgotten Clara's allowance after all these years? Armand wasn't pleased to see us either. He covered that up by talking too much, and practically pushing us out of the door. But the genial, generous nephew

137

veneer was cracked quite a lot. He's not used to making a mid-week visit, but something brought him down tonight. What? Anyway, I've swiped a pile of Clara's letters and we'll study those presently."

"If you can stop talking long enough," Philip said pleasantly. He put his hand on hers and gave it a friendly squeeze. "It was quite an ordeal, wasn't it?"

Lydia sighed and leaned back. "I'm talking too much, just as Armand was. Only he behaved as if he were cold."

"He was scared to death," said Philip.

"Scared!"

"Couldn't you see?"

"But what of? Blandina? I admit that if I had an aunt like that living in an hotel I'd very happily leave her there. I don't believe she forgot Clara's allowance. She just decided that, having a place like this to come to, she'd wash her hands of her poor old sister."

"She acts as if she's lived at Greenhill for years," Philip observed.

"Oh, no, she's just that kind of woman. Takes over immediately she arrives. Tell me, what did you do while I was upstairs with Clara?"

"There wasn't much I could do. That fellow Jules never let me out of his sight."

"Really! Unwritten orders?"

"I should imagine so. I took a look in several rooms—I must have seemed an unmannerly snooper. He politely interpreted that what I was looking for was the cloakroom, and showed me in."

Lydia giggled. "Serves you right."

"I wanted to get upstairs, but it wasn't possible."

"Why? To look in all those empty bedrooms?" Lydia's voice was a little fearful. She was thinking again of her fantasy of the mummifying old women.

"Might have been interesting," Philip said thoughtfully. "Armand is no doubt a man of secrets. He looks to me like the kind of solicitor who should have been struck off the roll years ago."

"Aurora wouldn't have stayed with a man like that!" Lydia exclaimed.

"But we don't know Aurora very well either, do we? Well, perhaps I'm wrong. I suppose you hadn't a chance to find out how that cry for help got in Clara's letter."

"No. I could only hint at it, and Clara seemed quite bewildered. If she did write it she's forgotten. She's not dying, Philip. At least, I wouldn't think so. And now they think we're calling again they'll be pretty careful. But supposing. . . ."

She stopped, unwilling to put her thought into words.

"Yes?"

"Supposing they did want her to die. Why? She's a completely destitute old woman. They haven't a thing to gain."

"I know. It doesn't make sense. Nevertheless, we're going to make another call tonight. We're distant relatives of Clara's, and we're anxious about her. We want to be assured by her doctor that she's not seriously ill. What do you say? Doctor Neave, isn't it? Someone in the village will tell us where to find him."

"Yes," said Lydia eagerly. "That's exactly what we must do."

It was not to be expected that a doctor would divulge much information about his patient to what appeared to be a pair of complete strangers. But at least this visit gave them the opportunity to sum up the man whom Blandina and Armand had decided to call in, to see whether or not he appeared to be sensible and trustworthy.

Doctor Neave, in the small, dark, cluttered surgery into which they were shown, was an elderly, rather vague person with a kindly face.

He listened to their story, and said, "You understand, this isn't strictly etiquette. Your aunt—she is your aunt, I take it?"

"Distantly," said Philip.

"Ah yes. Well—ah—I diagnosed the trouble as a small cerebral hæmorrhage, in other words, a slight stroke, with symptoms such as nausea and confusion. At her age, of course —well—ah—none of us lives for ever, eh? But with care she'll be perfectly all right. Fortunately there's no paralysis.

139

Normally I'd have put a case like that in hospital, but she seems to be getting such excellent care where she is, I feel one couldn't do better. I gather a holiday abroad is proposed when she is well enough to travel."

"Yes. So Aunt Clara mentioned," Philip said easily. "I suppose you've attended Mr. Villette—and his aunts—for some years, Doctor?"

"No, actually I haven't. Luckily for them—not, of course for me—" the laboured joke brought a twinkle to the old man's faded eyes, "they haven't often needed a doctor. The last time was several years ago."

"Was that for one of the aunts?"

"Yes. It was. Let me see, what was her name. Honoria, Hortense, Hannah—that was it, Hannah. She had a long-standing heart ailment and died. But no, I haven't been called in often. Of course, as you know, the family doesn't live at Greenhill a great deal. They're rather cosmopolitan, I gather."

"Lucky things," Lydia sighed. "Money no object. Just as well for Armand, of course, since he's so aunt-ridden."

"Only one dead and gone aunt," Lydia said, when they were back in the car. "Then the others Armand mentioned must have died somewhere else."

"That's enough of that," Philip said firmly. "We can't clutter up things with ancient corpses."

"All the same, Armand must have kept very silent about Aunt Hannah's death, because the postmistress didn't know of it. What a honey that little doctor is. I'm sure he'll do all he can for Clara, won't he? And if it's a stroke, there's no one to blame, is there? She's not being poisoned, or anything melodramatic like that. What do we do now, Philip?"

"Have dinner in the first pub we come to, and read those letters you helped yourself to."

The waiter in the cosy roadside hotel looked curiously at them as he tried to set down their plates among the litter of crumpled letters spread over the table.

Most of the letters were in Miss Wilberforce's usual rambling style, and addressed to herself. Lydia put them on one

140

side to study later. She searched for the one in the strange handwriting, and when she opened it she gasped. For it was from Aurora.

It read,

"Dear Miss Wilberforce,

"I am enclosing five pounds which is all I can possibly send you. This will help you out until you have arranged something with the National Health people. Do go to them at once." (The last word was underlined.) "Don't come here."

It was signed "Aurora Hawkins". The date was six weeks ago.

"Why did Aurora feel she had to send her money? What obligation was she under? How is she mixed up in all this, Philip? Just by being Armand's secretary?" The letter was just one more thing to baffle Lydia.

"Secretaries don't usually have to pay bribes to clients," Philip said. "Does one thing occur to you about this letter? It's dated about the time that Blandina moved from her hotel down to the country."

"Well, of course. That's when poor Clara's allowance stopped. But why should Aurora feel responsible? Really, this is too complicated."

"For me, too," Philip confessed. "I only have one idea. When we get back to London let's advertise in the personal column for friends of Blandina's. Surely she must have had some friends."

"How can they help us?"

"Well, for one thing, they can tell us what she looked like."

"Philip! Are you suggesting that terrifying old woman might not be Blandina?"

"I'm not sure what I'm suggesting. But there's no harm in doing this, is there?" He began to write on the back of one of the tattered letters. "'Paxton Blandina: Can anyone give an old friend any idea of her whereabouts. Have not been able to contact her since she left London some weeks ago.' How's that?"

"Splendid."

"She must have had some friends," Philip repeated. "I enquired about her at the hotel, but all they could tell me was about the nephew who took her out to tea sometimes."

"Armand, of course."

"The irrepressible Armand."

"He's after her money, Philip. Even though he seems to have plenty of his own. He doesn't want poor old Clara to get any."

"At the moment neither of them seems likely to get any. She looked as if she would live forever, didn't she?"

"But she must be Blandina, Philip. She's always talking to Clara about their childhood. And she's bossy, the way Clara said."

"Clara's memory is pretty bad. And it's easy enough to spin a story out of just a few correct details, especially to someone a little weak-witted like Clara."

"Philip!" Now the cold wind was blowing over Lydia again. The exciting tense evening had left her exhausted. She had no resources left with which to dispel this wave of fear. "You're thinking of that unidentified body again," she said, in a horrified whisper.

"I don't think such a long chance would interest the police at all," Philip said reflectively. "We must get one or two more facts straight. And we have a little time now. We're due to call in at Greenhill in two or three days, remember? To give them that nasty little surprise for which they'll have to be prepared. So they can't afford just yet to play any tricks. Cheer up, darling. Let's have a bottle of wine. The rest of the evening is ours."

"Ours!" echoed Lydia ironically. For how could it be, when Clara Wilberforce, shrunken, pathetic and determinedly cheerful, sitting up trustingly in the comfortable bed in the comfortable room remained so firmly in her mind. And not only Clara, Aurora, too, with her mysterious part in this queer play. The servant Jules, suave, silent and watchful. Armand, a little grotesquely coy, wringing his hands as if he were cold. And Blandina—or the two Blandinas—one the severe hostess, un-

142

welcoming and hostile, long-nosed and autocratic, the other a ghost, unknown, bewildered, forgotten. . . .

It was after midnight when they got back to London. Lydia had dozed, and woke only when the car stopped.

"Here we are, my love. I'll come up with you."

"Will you," said Lydia sleepily. "I'd adore that."

"Well, that's better," he said, grinning down at her.

She became fully awake. "What did I say?"

"Just what you should have. I say, if you can't walk straight I'll have to carry you. We don't want our friend and neighbour sticking her nose out at this hour."

Lydia giggled. "Don't worry. This is her sleeping-like-a-log time. Of course you're not going to carry me," she added wistfully.

But she let him put his arm firmly round her waist, and with exaggerated caution they climbed the stone stairs.

Lydia was happy again. Her drowsiness and the space they had put between themselves and Greenhill had reduced the problem to something a great deal less pressing and personal. After all, as Philip had once pointed out, nothing tangible had happened. No one was hurt, or seemingly in desperate trouble, or dead. . . . Except the aged Hannah, legitimately, of a long-standing heart ailment.

Outside the door of her flat she groped in her bag, now as bulging and untidy as Miss Wilberforce's, with its clutter of correspondence.

But Philip's hand was suddenly on her arm. He was indicating the not-quite-closed door.

Someone was in there!

Aurora's mysterious friend?

"Oh! What do we do?" Lydia gasped.

Philip didn't answer. He gave the door a sharp push, at the same time groping inside for the light switch. The light sprang on, but the door refused to open more than six inches. Something heavy lay against it.

Pushing slowly and carefully, Philip at last edged his way in. His voice, exaggeratedly calm, came out to Lydia.

"It's June Birch. She's hurt."

143

In a moment Lydia was inside bending over June, while Philip quickly switched on lights in the rest of the flat and checked to see that the intruder was no longer there.

June was just recovering consciousness. She was dressed in pyjamas and a cotton housecoat. She frowned at the light and moaned.

"O-oh! You've come at last. I thought——"

"Take it easy," said Philip. He had a glass of brandy in one hand, and raising June a little with his free arm he persuaded her to swallow some.

Lydia rushed to get cushions and a wet cloth. The bump on June's head was startlingly visible.

"Someone—knocked me out," she managed to say at last, grinning ruefully. "Gosh! That's some headache I've got."

"Did you see who it was?" Philip asked.

"No! Not a whisker of him! I thought I heard someone moving up here—oh, ever so softly, quite late—what's the time now?"

"Half-past twelve."

"Then, my goodness, it was only ten minutes ago. You've just missed him."

"Oh, lord!" Philip exclaimed angrily.

Lydia had a rather fearful sense of relief. Supposing— but never mind. It hadn't happened. It was June who had suffered.

"I came up with my key to catch him red-handed. At least, to get a look at him. But as soon as I opened the door the lights went out, and wham! I got this on my head."

She slumped back. "Gosh! Only ten minutes ago! He's nipped down the back stairs, of course."

"Has anything been disturbed?" Lydia asked Philip.

"Of course it has. Everything's upside down. But whether he got what he wanted is another thing."

"What would he want?" Lydia asked fearfully.

"I don't know. I only make a guess. The pendant, of course."

"Aurora!" whispered Lydia.

"Come off it," said June feebly. "That was a man-sized wallop I got."

144

"She might have had a man with her," said Philip slowly. "Or it might have been just one man alone."

"Armand!"

"Perhaps. How do we know? Let's make June more comfortable. Do you think you can sit up? We'll move you on to the couch. Then I think—whatever you two may feel—it's a case for the police."

At that June sat up sharply. She clutched her head, but managed to say very definitely, "Don't be daft! The police will just treat this as an ordinary burglary, and we'll never find out who this guy is. It's not a burglary," she added soberly. "It's part of this crazy mystery about Aurora. And I might be wrong, but I've got a feeling if you call the police you'll never see Aurora again."

"What an extraordinary thing to say!" Lydia exclaimed.

June grinned wryly. "Maybe that bump on my head has sent me crazy. But that's what I think. And I want to meet up with this irresistible lover. Among other things, I've got a score to settle with him."

Philip said slowly, but with an excited gleam in his eye, "She may be right, Lydia. The police at this stage—hell, I don't know. Are they going to listen to a lot of airy-fairy nonsense about old women in the country and disappearing brides? They like facts. Stolen jewellery. Bodies. . . . I'd like to see what this advertisement about Blandina brings. And anyway we haven't lost the pendant. I've got it in my pocket."

June made a motion of clapping her hands. "Ha! The villain foiled!" she declared triumphantly.

18

"Aurora! Are you still sleeping?"

The familiar voice, close to her ear, stirred her reluctantly from deep slumber. She didn't want to wake. She didn't know

145

why she wanted so much to cling to unconsciousness. She could hear birds singing, and the light against her eyes told her that it was morning and the sun was shining. Once she had loved to wake to a sunny morning.

"No! I'm awake," she murmured.

"Good girl. Look! It's a fine day and we're moving."

"Moving?"

"I told you last night."

"Did you? I don't remember. No, you didn't tell me."

She was coming slowly awake, sitting up in bed, seeing the now familiar room and his familiar head on the pillow.

The room with the locked door she was to leave behind, since he said so, but this face with the narrowed, amused eyes, the tilted eyebrows, the half smile that teased her, this face that she knew like a well-loved map, was coming with her. Every morning when she awoke she would find it on the pillow beside her. Blurred with sleep and languor, for a moment she was completely happy.

"Darling!" she murmured.

He smiled radiantly.

"That's right, my sweet. That's how I like to hear you talk."

She frowned a little. "Don't I always?"

"Not always. Not lately. Sometimes you've behaved as if you've hated the sight of me."

"Hated you! But if I had, I wouldn't have come away with you that night. Would I? Just as I was."

"Just as you were was sufficient, angel."

She smiled reminiscently. "You wouldn't even let me go back to pack a bag."

"I was afraid you might change your mind again."

"Oh, no. Not then. It was always you I loved. You knew that."

"So I did." He gathered her into his arms, pulling her down against his hard chest. "And I love you, too. When you're a good girl. Remember?"

It was strange the way she couldn't quite wake up. Her limbs were heavy and her head felt dull, as if she had had too much to drink, but was not quite drunk. Yet she didn't want

146

to shake off this dullness because if she did there were vague frightening things that were no longer dreamlike. Things such as telephone calls, and voices shouting at her, and the key turning in the lock of her door. . . .

It was much better this way, being heavy and far-off, not even minding that the way he pressed her against him hurt her breasts, as if they were crushed inside the cage of his ribs.

"You said we were going somewhere?"

"Yes, I did. You've got to get up and pack."

"By train?"

"Perhaps."

"Oh, darling! We've caught so many trains. I'm really terribly tired."

"Do you want me to leave you behind?"

"Don't be silly! Of course I don't."

His smiling eyes caressed her. "Then wake up, Aurora darling. And be a good girl. No tricks."

"Tricks?"

Suddenly he pushed her from him.

"You know damn well what I mean. I think half the time you put on this being stupid act. Or didn't you take your pills last night?"

"Yes, I did. You watched me."

"They're good for your nerves. You know that, don't you. You've been quite ill, you know, and I don't want to have to put you in hospital. I'm looking after you as well as I can. I'm looking after both of us." His brilliant gaze pierced into her. "Aren't I?" he asked significantly, and then gave his soft laugh.

"All right, angel. Don't worry about it. Kiss me."

Automatically she bent her head to obey. But as his arms tightened round her she began to shiver. It was not because of the pain of her crushed breasts, but because of that now familiar fear. His arms held this terribly frightening enchantment, and she could not escape. She was mesmerised, she would take the pills for her nerves, or anything else he told her to do. She knew that she was helpless against him, and so long as he wanted her she didn't care that he dominated her.

147

Yet when he had left the room, saying he was going to get coffee, and she got tiredly out of bed to sit at the dressing-table, the fear swept over her again.

For the face looking back at her from the mirror had changed so much. It was quite colourless, and rather puffy, with dark hollows round her eyes, and her eyes themselves dull and heavy-lidded. Her hair, too, was limp and flat against her head, all the life gone out of it.

He only loved her when she was beautiful. She knew that. Her beauty had been her weapon over him. So how could he love this white-faced travesty of herself?

And if he didn't love her, what was going to happen to her?

Footsteps outside the door telling her he was coming back made her seize the hairbrush and hurriedly try to brush some life into her hair.

But no one came in for a moment. There were voices instead. She could hear what was apparently the end of a conversation.

"But it's my wife, I told you last night. I have to go. I must go."

"It can wait a day or two."

"But if I don't go immediately she won't come back. I'll lose trace of her."

"My dear chap, if she's left you, you know the reason. It's a waste of time your pursuing her. And I can't spare you at present. You know that damned well."

"Then I shall go in any case."

"I don't think so. I really don't think you will, you know."

The voices stopped. The door opened. The girl at the mirror began to tremble.

19

The woman behind the reception desk in the Bayswater hotel bridled a little when Philip confidingly leaned across the desk to her.

"I was talking to you the other day, Miss——"

"Perkins. Miss Perkins. Yes, I remember you. You were asking about your aunt, Mrs. Paxton. Did you find her?"

"Actually, no. At least, I don't think so."

The woman looked mystified. "You mean you're not sure?"

"Not entirely. Can you describe exactly what she looked like?"

"Well—she was just an old woman, not especially conspicuous. Grey hair, of course. No identifying marks, as the police call them."

"Too bad," said Philip pleasantly. "Was she tall?"

"Yes, quite. Held herself well for an old lady."

Philip suddenly had an idea. He took a pencil from his pocket and began to sketch swiftly on the desk pad.

"Did she look like this?"

Miss Perkins studied the sketch and giggled nervously.

"O-oh! What a big nose. No, I don't think her nose was that big."

"But she did have a long nose?"

"Well, yes, I think you could say it was quite long. What are you getting at, if I may ask?"

"I'm just trying to satisfy myself about a point that's worrying me. Have you ever seen this before?"

Miss Perkins started back as he laid the gold pendant on the desk.

"Why, yes, I have. That's Mrs. Paxton's. I've often seen her wearing it. Well, if you've got that, you've found your aunt, haven't you? Or"—her eyes popped—"how else did you get it?"

"That's another story," Philip said. "Thank you very much, Miss Perkins. You've been quite a help."

"But what are you trying to do? Is it some plot? If it is," Miss Perkins was calling after him, her voice sharp with frustration, "why don't you get the police?"

"Can't tell you now. Watch the daily newspapers."

In the street Philip went into a telephone box and dialled the number of Aurora's flat.

"Hullo!" came Lydia's excited voice. "Is that you, Philip?"

"Yes. What's happened?"

149

"How do you know something has?"

"By your voice, stupid." He didn't add that already he knew every inflection of her voice, when she was happy, when she was tired, when she suffered from disappointment or remorse, or even when she coolly hid her feelings. All the little things he hadn't known about Aurora. . . .

"I've had a telephone call from someone who has seen our advertisement."

"Who is he? What does he say?"

Philip, fresh from his illuminating and disturbing interview with Miss Perkins at the Bayswater hotel, was almost as tense with excitement as Lydia.

"He says he has a café on the Portsmouth Road. He doesn't know Blandina, but about two months ago an old woman called by that name stopped for tea. At least, Blandina was a passenger in a car with two other people. He said he particularly remembered the name because it was unusual."

"Did you get his exact address?"

"Of course, what do you think!" came Lydia's cool voice. "When do we go down?"

"Now. I'll be round. How's June?"

"She's got two gorgeous black eyes. She says she's fine, otherwise, and is rather enjoying herself. I'm doing her shopping because she doesn't want people to think she's been beaten up. How long will you be?"

"Fifteen minutes. If you can stop talking. I've got a hunch we haven't much time to lose."

"Good. That will give me time to rush out for June's lunch," Lydia answered serenely. "Don't go without me."

"Don't go without me. . . ." The words echoed in Philip's head as he impatiently edged his way across London through the exasperatingly slow traffic. If she only knew, she had become, in these weeks, more than a habit with him. He had grown accustomed to her intensely alive face, her short, ruffled hair, her eager response, her impulsive and reckless kindness. She had kindled something in him that responded to a different kind of beauty from Aurora's exquisite perfection. But he made mistakes, choosing the wrong moment to tell her so,

150

getting tied up with his sense of loyalty to Aurora whom, after all, he had been going to marry.

His thoughts had become incoherent by the time he reached the flat in St. John's Wood. He sat honking the horn until Lydia came flying out, hatless as usual, her cheeks pink.

"Just made it. June's staying out of sight, although I don't think she'd mind seeing you. She's more of a sport than I'd have thought at first. She's keeping her ears open again today for any suspicious sounds. But there won't be any, after last night. I should think the fellow would have the sense to keep away. He's probably been reading the papers to see if June's body was discovered." She gave him a quick rueful glance. "I'm talking too much again."

"Go ahead," said Philip mildly. "So long as you can stop to tell me where we're going."

"I'm sorry. If I don't talk this awful excitement, or whatever it is, just swells up inside me. We've got to look for a caravan café on the side of the road just before we get to Guildford. This man only rang half an hour ago."

"What did he sound like?"

"Rather slow and solemn. The philosopher type, I should think. Observing life from the side of a main highway. Did you find out anything this morning?"

Philip nodded and tossed his information over casually. "The pendant is Blandina's. Or was."

"Blandina's! Then—do you suppose Armand stole it? Or borrowed it? And that's why it's important to get it back."

"We might go on down to Greenhill and find out. What do you say? Tell him he doesn't need to go round hitting women on the head to get back his bit of jewellery."

"And demand to know what is in all those bedrooms?" Lydia said breathlessly.

"I don't know about the bedrooms. But we can try some bluff. I've a notion they're so deadly serious they won't be able to stand bluff."

"Armand will be in London."

"I've a feeling he won't. I rang his office just after I rang you and there was no answer. I think M'sieur Armand might be taking a day at home today. It's not surprising he sacked his secretary, you know. She might have been answering too many awkward questions."

Lydia let out her breath in a large sigh. "I don't think I can stand so much all at once."

"Don't worry," Philip reassured her. "We'll have a double whisky with the postmistress. It might even make her remember the deceased Aunt Hannah. When we've done with resurrecting aunts, we'll——"

"What?" Lydia asked fearfully.

"I don't know. But I think somehow, strange as it may seem, we'll have found Aurora."

The café proprietor was a lean, tall, lugubrious person who was absorbed in a book, and seemed loath to put it aside. He did so at last, carefully marking his place, and asked what they wanted.

"Tea," said Lydia blithely. "We'll talk while we have it."

The man was very perceptive. "You're the people who've been asking about the old lady!"

"That's right," Philip answered. "Can you tell us anything?"

"Nothing except the name. That, being unusual, stuck in my mind. And the fact that she seemed lost, sort of. I worried about her a bit. I live here by myself and I notice my customers. Anything different strikes me. I got this old woman on my mind for a bit, and then when I read your ad. this morning I thought to myself, I bet it's that old woman they're wanting. It's the unusual name, see. Blandina. I haven't come across it before, even in a book, and I'm a great reader. Milk and sugar, madam?"

"Thank you," said Lydia. She admired the deft way he poured the tea, economical with his movements, no slopping in the saucer. The book he had been reading, she noticed, was the *Diary of a Country Parson*. In his own way he was as memorable as Blandina.

Philip produced the rough sketch he had made.

"Was this old woman anything like this?"

The man studied it, his head on one side thoughtfully.

152

"Sorry, sir. You've had your trip for nothing, if that's the party you're enquiring about. It's not her."

"Are you sure?" Lydia exclaimed.

"Quite sure, madam. I know it was night time, but the light was on in the car and I saw her quite clearly. She wasn't like that. She was more crumpled, if you know what I mean. The way old people get when the flesh sinks back into their body. Consuming itself, you might say. This old lady was like that, and sort of scared and lost, as if she didn't know how she'd come to be in the back of that car."

"What make of car was it? Did you notice?"

"Certainly I did." The man drew himself up, his powers of observation challenged. "I don't often have Jaguars pulling up here. They're pub traffic, usually. They and the Bentleys and the Rolls."

"And who was this old lady with?" Philip asked softly.

"A man and a girl. The girl was pretty. She seemed to be comforting the old woman. I got the feeling they'd stopped for tea, unobtrusively, if you follow me, because the old lady needed some sort of stimulation. But they wanted it quick and without fuss, perhaps without being noticed too much. Yes, that's how I saw it. The man's name was Armand. I remember that. The girl said it. Both unusual names, in a way. But the Blandina one struck me."

"Thank you," said Philip. "That helps us a lot."

"You think that's the party you're looking for, sir?"

"I think so, without a doubt."

"I couldn't tell you where they were heading for. And I'm sure the old woman didn't know either. She was saying something about a strange road. I read too much, of course, being on my own all the time. But my fancy was she was being kidnapped. Well, you know. Taken somewhere she wouldn't like when she got there. One of those old women's homes she didn't want to go to, most likely. More tea, sir?"

"No, thank you. I'm afraid you do read too much, or your imagination is a bit vivid."

The man nodded sagely. "I expect you're right. I watch all those cars whirling past, night and day, and I wonder where

153

in hell they're all going, and if they know themselves. So then I get my nose in a book about the old days, nice slow jogging in carriages a few miles at a time. That would be the life for me. You'd know where you were going then. Not whirled away into the night like that poor old Blandina. More tea, madam?"

"No, thank you very much. It was very good. We have to go on. We're in a hurry, too. But we do know where we're going. At least——" Lydia hesitated. Nothing could be more ordinary than this caravan pulled in at the roadside, with its counter flap down, than the cars speeding past, the clouds moving slowly over an early summer sky, the smell of hot sweet tea and petrol fumes, and smoke from a distant bonfire. Yet suddenly everything seemed completely unreal, as unreal as it must have been to a bewildered old woman, crumpled and nondescript, being hurried away in the night to some unknown destination.

Lydia began practising her friendly and casual smile some time before they reached Greenhill. As the miles slid away it became a little wobbly, and her heart was beating unevenly again. She rehearsed out loud,

"It's us again, would you believe it! How is Aunt Clara? And Aunt Blandina, you must have missed this piece of jewellery. Did you know dear nephew Armand had helped himself to it, and given it to someone else's bride?" She broke off. "But Philip! Who *is* Aurora's husband?"

"I should be surprised if she has one," Philip said, with a quiet grimness that effectively dispatched Lydia's frivolity.

"You mean, she's the decoy, or something?"

"She's in this, I'm sure. How, I don't know. But we'll find that out today, if I'm not mistaken."

Lydia hugged her arms round herself. She refused to start trembling again. It was so weak.

"If Aurora isn't married, if she's living in sin, that will be the end as far as Daddy is concerned. Even if it's been done at the point of a gun, I don't think he'd approve. Oh, gosh! We're almost there."

"If you're nervous, will you stay in the car?"

"Stay in the car! What *are* you talking about?"

Philip grinned, and made his familiar gesture of laying his hand over hers.

"Do you know something, Lydia? I didn't tell you before. It seemed disloyal. But Aurora asked me to marry her—well, before I'd got round to doing the asking myself."

Lydia looked at him in astonishment. "But surely, allowing for good manners and all that, surely a man doesn't have to accept a woman!"

"Of course not. I was crazy about her. I would have got round to it—it just happened a little sooner this way."

Lydia was sceptical. "I don't think that's true. I think she was afraid of losing you."

"No, not that. It's more likely she was trying to escape from something that frightened her. I offered as good a solution as any. And I really was crazy about her. A beautiful woman always knocks me silly. Beware of that in the future—give me a sharp kick when I start behaving oddly."

"My kick has quite a punch to it," Lydia murmured, mixing her metaphors happily.

In the future, he had said. After this nightmare visit, being made in brilliant sunshine in mid-afternoon, was over. . . .

The house looked very quiet, with all its windows shut. But that was not unusual. It had never betrayed signs of life. One rang the doorbell, and presently footsteps announced that someone was at home.

Lydia, standing very close to Philip on the doorstep, waited. The lawns needed cutting, she noticed. Jules must have been too busy in the house lately to attend to his gardening duties. It was strange that such a small part of the garden was cultivated. Beyond that the grass and weeds, pushing up among elderly rose bushes and shrubs, grew rank.

"No one's coming," she whispered.

He put his finger on the bell again, and held it there a moment. They could hear it ringing far off. But still it brought no footsteps. The door remained shut. The windows were closed and blank.

"They said they were going away as soon as Miss Wilberforce

was well enough," Lydia said. "Do you think they've gone, whether she's well or not?"

"Cleared out before we called again? Surely they're not that scared of us!"

"Good heavens! Supposing they are. They must have awfully guilty consciences. Why? Philip, we've got to find out."

"I agree," he said tersely.

"Then why are we standing here? No one's going to open that door. Let's go round to the back. If there's no one home, you know——"

"I know. We break in."

"But we've got to find something unlocked. I expect the place is bolted like the Tower of London."

"If they've left in a hurry they might have slipped up on that. Let's see."

Ten minutes later they were inside the house. A loose bolt on a pantry window had given way to their joint pressure and enabled them to slip quietly inside.

But now Lydia was overcome with fear. Supposing, after all, the house was not empty, but that its occupants were deliberately not answering the door to callers. Supposing, at the next turn of the passage, they came abruptly on Blandina, silent and terrifying.

The large kitchen showed the remains of a hasty breakfast. Dishes were left untidily in the sink, there were broken egg-shells, and the remains of a glass of milk. Philip swiftly counted four cups. "Clara, Blandina, Armand and Jules," he said. "Jules obviously eats with the family when they all eat in the kitchen."

"There's this glass of milk."

"They might have forced some of that down poor old Clara. She'd need building up for the journey. Come on. Let's look in the other rooms."

The hall, the dining-room and the drawing-room, the only part of the ground floor that Lydia had seen on her previous visits, were the same as usual, except that the curtains were drawn in the dining-room, making it dim and gloomy. It was

156

a chilly room. Lydia shivered, but had no time to linger for Philip was calling her. "I say, come and look in here."

He had opened a door farther along the hall, and was looking in at a library, cold, dark and dusty.

"No one's been in here for years, by the look of it. It seems to me the main rooms have been used and kept tidy, and the rest of the house shut up. I shouldn't be surprised if there were no servants here at all except Jules."

"Because they couldn't get them or because they couldn't afford them?"

"Or because they preferred not to have any strangers about?"

"I was told it was the cook's day off," Lydia said.

Philip was sceptical.

"A long day, probably. My guess is that Armand doesn't come here very much and when he does strangers aren't encouraged. Let's go upstairs."

Lydia hesitated a moment, wondering how he could leap up the long flight of stairs so confidently. Then she resolutely followed him, telling herself that she had been longing, after all, to get a look into all those closed rooms.

One door led into Blandina's, and another into Miss Wilberforce's. The others. . . . Supposing the house were not empty after all. They hadn't really stopped to listen, to hear whether anyone stirred, or to see if anyone secretly watched them.

"Come on," called Philip. "You know whose these rooms were. The grandfather clock is still going, anyway."

Yes, that was the measured sound that accentuated the silence. The slow tick-tock that she had fancifully thought was ticking the sick Blandina's life away. But Blandina was not reduced yet to counting the seconds. She was superbly indifferent to them. It was poor Clara whose time was running out.

The first door Philip opened was that of Blandina's room.

Involuntarily Lydia hesitated on the threshold. She was so sure the wide bed would contain the old lady, her nose poking skywards, her sharp black eyes refusing stubbornly to close.

"What are you scared of?" said Philip. "There's no one here."

157

The bed was tidy, the heavy counterpane drawn up over any dishevelled bedclothes. The wardrobe, which Philip had opened, was empty of clothes. There were no brushes or cosmetics on the dressing-table. There was, indeed, little sign that the room had been so recently inhabited. A few hairpins and a grey hair or two in the old-fashioned hair tidy, a slightly dented cushion on a chair, and one of the floor rugs a little crooked. That was all.

Miss Wilberforce's room was much the same, except that there was a half-empty glass of lemon and barley water on the bedside table, and the bed had scarcely been tidied. She must have been got up at the last minute when the car was ready.

The famous black handbag had gone. Had she noticed it was a good deal lighter and slimmer?

"This is where I spilt the letters," Lydia said, because some normal conversation had to break the terrifying silence. "I wonder if I missed any. I couldn't look round very much with Blandina watching like a hawk."

She got down on her hands and knees to peer under the chest of drawers, then lifted the heavy valance of the bed.

"Oh, there's one!" she cried. "Oh, it's just one she's written to herself. No, it's not! No, it's not, Philip! There's something else stuck in the envelope. Look! It's in different hand-writing. It——"

Her voice died away. The clumsily printed words, "Don't stay here! They're all murderers," seemed to quiver before her eyes.

"Philip! Who's written this?"

"Melodrama!" he murmured softly.

"It will be the person who added the postscript to that letter to me," Lydia exclaimed, answering her own question.

"Most likely. Keep that. And come on."

He was impatient to see what else was to be found, conscious of time growing more and more vital.

But the remainder of the rooms told little. There was one that seemed as if it had been recently occupied because of its lack of dust. The others were in a similar condition to the

158

ibrary downstairs, closed, chilly, slightly musty smelling, untouched for a long time.

Except one round the turn of the passage, and that was locked. Philip tried in vain to look through the keyhole. He rattled at the knob. All the doors in the house were solidly made of oak of the best workmanship. It was impossible to try to break in. Besides, what would be there, but more mustiness and dust?

"In the best fairy-tale traditions," Lydia said shakily. "The door that mustn't be opened. Oh, Philip, let's go."

"Scared?" he asked quizzically.

"Yes, I am. And I'm not ashamed of it. I feel—ghoulish."

All at once there was a distant thud downstairs. She leapt into his arms.

"Steady!" he said. "Do you want to wait here?"

"No! I'm coming with you."

They hurried down the stairs.

"Is anyone home?" Philip called loudly.

In the kitchen a kitten miaoued. Philip laughed with relief. He found the tabby-striped offender and picked it up. It began to purr with a volume of sound completely out of proportion to its meagre body.

"It's followed us in through the window. Let's give it the rest of Clara's milk."

"And then let's go," Lydia begged. "There's nothing here. Frankly, I can't stand the place. I hope I never see it again."

Philip poured milk into a saucer and watched the kitten lapping.

"All right," he said at last. "But we'll have a word with the postmistress on the way."

The sun shone brightly over the strange, untended garden with its tidy centre—which was like the house with its dusted and polished pool of rooms flanked by the undusted airless ones. The rhododendrons were bursting into crimson bloom. A thrush was standing in a listening attitude on the lawn, and the kitten which had followed them out crouched with comical intensity, a miniature potential thunderbolt.

The brightness of the afternoon made the silent house with

159

its untold story even more eerily mystifying. Looking up at the first-floor windows, it was possible to identify the one that belonged to the locked room. But it looked exactly the same as the others, blank and shut.

"But we haven't finished with this," Philip reminded her. "We're in it now, whether we like it or not."

Lydia shivered and begged again, "Let's go."

The postmistress offered them tea, and told them about the fast car that had gone through the village early that morning.

"I was just making my cup of tea," she said. "If my kitchen didn't face over the street I wouldn't have seen it, it was gone that quick."

"Could you see who was in it?"

"No. It went by too fast. Well, now, what a disappointment, you coming all the way down to visit your friends and there being no one home. Are they close friends of yours?"

She peered at them with her faded, lavender-coloured eyes.

"No. Not particularly."

The postmistress, who was a genial person, gave a snort of laughter and said, "Then I can say my piece about them folding their tents like the Arabs and silently stealing away. They do, you know. We know nothing about their comings and goings. They don't shop in the village, or even have a char from hereabouts. But there, you can't know everyone's family history, can you? Plenty of town people have country houses in these parts. They change hands from time to time, and you don't hear much about it. I understood these particular people were on the Continent a lot. I'm sorry I can't help you more."

Philip drove very fast out of the village. Lydia didn't ask him why he was hurrying so much. She was a little afraid to be told. But all at once she said intensely, "I know Aurora's in that locked room. I know."

"Sleeping for a hundred years?" Philip cocked an eyebrow at her. But he didn't laugh. Nor did he deny her fantastic statement. Instead, he slowed down the car.

"You know, there was a ledge along those top windows. I rather think I could work my way along and get in that room through the window."

"Could you? Could you really?"

He smiled at her eagerness. Now he stopped the car. "I believe you're encouraging me to break my neck!"

"Don't be absurd! But supposing Aurora is there—I mean, it might be important to hurry."

"Let's go back," said Philip.

Lydia stood long enough in the garden to see Philip emerge from a window and work his careful way along the ledge to the safety of the next window.

"Nothing to it," he called down to her. "Easier than climbing a coconut palm."

Then he eased up the window and began to climb inside.

Lydia didn't wait any longer. Nervous as she was of the dim, eerie house, its only sound the ticking of the grandfather clock, like a ponderous heart, she raced up the stairs, arriving breathlessly at the other side of the locked door.

"Are you in there? Philip! Have you found anything? Open the door!"

Philip rattled the handle. After a moment he said, "Can't. There's no key. It's been locked from the outside and the key taken away. There's nothing here, by the way, except an empty bed."

Lydia sagged against the wall. "Then why is the door locked? To shut in a ghost?"

There were sounds from within as Philip opened drawers and cupboards. Then his voice came back, low and reflective.

"I believe you're right, Lydia. There is a ghost. Now I'm going back the way I came, so run along downstairs." His voice rose a little, tautly. "Get out of this damned place!"

She obeyed without speaking. She ran down the stairs as if the great clock, the only alive thing in the house, were swinging ponderously after her, its pendulum thrust out like a long grasping arm. She literally tumbled out into the cool garden, and looked up to see Philip completing his precarious climb.

Presently he joined her. She didn't immediately ask him what he had found. She clung to his arm with gratitude and relief.

"Were you scared?" he asked.

"Petrified."

"There's nothing to be frightened of now. There's no one there. All that's in that room is the dress Aurora was wearing the night she ran off. You remember? It was grey, thin stuff, like cobwebs. And her shoes. High-heeled bits of nonsense. Quite impractical for ordinary wear."

"Ordinary?" Lydia said faintly.

"One imagines she's decently equipped for other journeys."

"But why lock the door if that's all there is to hide?"

"I hardly know. Unless it's from habit. Come. We've got to get back to London before five o'clock." He added in explanation, "If that fellow Villette isn't in his office this time we go to the police."

"He won't be there," Lydia said fatalistically.

"If he has any business at all apart from——" Philip suddenly cleared his throat and finished mildly, "He can't completely neglect his business. He must leave instructions with someone."

On the steep, linoleum covered stairway leading up to Armand's office they encountered the postman.

"Office is closed up there," he said. "I've been trying to get an answer for two days now. You don't happen to know if they're away on holiday, do you? There's no notice up."

There were also three bottles of milk lined up forlornly outside the door.

"If they were on holiday one imagines they would notify the milkman," Philip said. "Afraid I can't help you. We were looking for Mr. Villette ourselves."

"Doesn't even have a girl in his office these days," the postman complained. "If you ask me, he's short of money and he's trying to get off with the trust funds!"

The man laughed loudly and clattered off down the stairs.

Lydia looked at the milk bottles and thought of a kitten lapping milk in an empty house in the country.

Philip seemed deep in thought. Suddenly he took her arm.

"Come on. Let's go to the nearest police station. It's better to have the law on our side before breaking down doors."

20

It took two hours and copious notes before they could convince the sergeant that there was real cause for their suspicions. He reprimanded them for not reporting the attempted burglary and assault on June Birch, but for the rest he kept muttering with the greatest scepticism, "Disappearing brides, kidnapped old women!"

He didn't care for it at all. If he let himself be taken in by it he would be laughed at by his superiors. But when Philip mentioned the torn newspaper and the paragraph about the unidentified body found beneath the cliffs along the Dorset coast, he grudgingly showed interest and said he would check to see whether identification had ever been established.

He had to go away to do this and when he came back he suggested that they might go and take a look at Armand Villette's offices. It seemed as if his activities, and particularly his files, might bear looking into.

"Don't suppose you noticed the number of that Jag?" he asked. "No? Well, let's go."

Lydia was asked to remain in the car while they went up the stairs to the office again. She seemed to wait a very long time. It was growing dark and the streets were emptying. Every sound was forlorn, the shriek of a car's brakes, the slow, dragging footsteps of an old woman passing, the rise and fall of a newsboy's call on the corner, somewhere a street fiddler playing a sentimental song. . . .

She wondered what she would tell Millicent whom she had promised to ring that evening. One either said nothing had happened, everything was fine, or one began to prepare her for—what? This silly obsession that somewhere in another locked room there was not merely Aurora's cobwebby dress and high-heeled shoes, but Aurora herself. . . .

When at last Philip returned, he was alone. He said tersely,

"I'm taking you home, darling. You can spend the evening with June, can't you?"

Lydia saw his grim face. "Why? What's the matter?"

"We found Armand Villette."

"What! Locked in, too? How did he explain that?"

"He didn't explain it. He was in no condition to do so—today or any other day."

"He's dead!" Lydia gasped.

Philip nodded. "The sergeant's sent for a doctor. But it's too late, I'm afraid. There's a fireplace full of burnt paper, and most of the files seem to have disappeared. He—or some-one—had been having quite a clean-up."

"You mean he's been murdered?"

"No, it's obviously suicide. Sleeping tablets, I think."

"But why? This makes nonsense of everything."

"Yes, it does."

"He was frightened of something last night," Lydia said, remembering the man's sudden unexpected arrival, his uneasy eyes, and the way he had pressed his hands together. "Supposing he isn't the villain after all."

Philip frowned thoughtfully. Then he got into the car and started the engine.

"I'm taking you home. Stay with June in the meantime. I'll ring if there's anything to report. Get yourself a good meal. You look like a starveling child."

But what did it matter how she looked? Lydia thought wildly. Where, anyway, did beauty get one, if one could take Aurora as an example?

It was the next day before the police traced the Jaguar to a garage in Brighton. It had been left there by a tall, good-looking man who said he was acting under instructions from the owner who would be out of England for an indefinite period. This person was obviously Jules, the gardener. He had been alone at the time.

After that the trail vanished.

A broadcast appeal had been made for relatives of Armand Villette, but no one seemed to be in the least interested in the stocky, grey-haired man, minus spectacles, eyelids firmly covering the round, rolling eyes, who lay waiting for someone to shed tears over him.

It was not possible to decide for whom the scrawled note found on his desk, written in a state of incoherent emotion, had been intended.

"Forgive me. I can't stand any more of this. It's too much. I'm caught in it too far." And again, *"Forgive me."*

A hasty preliminary enquiry into Armand Villette's life and practice as a solicitor was being made, but the most urgent thing was not to reconstruct Armand's life, but to trace the two old women, Blandina Paxton and Clara Wilberforce, seemingly spirited away in charge of the gardener Jules. And, of course, Aurora Hawkins who, if she was not actively involved in this abduction, could at least give the police a great deal of information. They would also try to trace the secretary who had followed Aurora, and who had had such a suspiciously brief stay in the office.

"They'll have gone to Aunt Honoria in Brittany," Lydia said, with certainty.

"But who would be taking them now Armand is dead?"

"Blandina, of course. She told me they would be going abroad."

"We're not even sure that woman is Blandina," Philip pointed out.

"Whoever she is, she knew her way around. I wouldn't be surprised if she mesmerised Armand into taking those sleeping tablets, especially when he had blundered."

"How had he blundered?"

"Why, in taking me down that first day, of course. I should never have been allowed to go there. Looking back, it does seem quite incredibly stupid, doesn't it? I wonder they didn't move there and then."

"Except that Clara was ill and couldn't be shifted. Her illness was genuine, I should think, as Doctor Neave told us."

"Then why that S O S in her letter?"

"Whoever sent that probably didn't believe her illness was genuine. Probably had reasons to be suspicious." Philip rubbed

165

his face tiredly. "You know, Lydia, that must have been Aurora."

"You mean she's been in that house all the time?"

"I don't know. It sounds crazy. But I wouldn't be surprised."

"Neither would I," Lydia admitted, for things were coming clear now. "She's been bribed or blackmailed into this. Those times she rang—she probably wanted help. Do you remember she began to say 'Come and get me'. She was probably interrupted by—well, by Blandina, I expect, who'd be enough to scare the wits out of anyone! And when she rang about the pendant, she was probably made to do that, too. I wonder why that pendant is so important."

"Of course it's important," Philip said harshly. "It's been identified as Blandina Paxton's. And supposing that old woman at the bottom of the cliffs is the real Blandina——"

"Then why on earth was Armand fool enough to let Aurora have the pendant?"

"He might not have known she had it. The old lady might have given it to her. She was in the car that night, you remember. The café man said so. Armand might only have discovered she had it when it was too late—I mean, after he had kidnapped her from her wedding."

"Kidnapped!"

"You don't suppose she would have gone with him willingly! He must have persuaded her, by some threat, to meet him just outside the village that night, and she went more or less innocently. After all, she had no luggage. She hadn't meant to run off that night."

"Then why didn't he make sure she had the pendant with her then?" Lydia demanded.

"At that stage he might not have known about it. But when she told him she had left incriminating evidence behind, as no doubt she did, in an effort to get away, he had to organise some means of getting it back."

"Why didn't he tell someone all this before he died? It's so useless to die this way." It was Lydia's turn to press her hands wearily against her face. "But where," she said, "is

166

Aurora now? Armand is no longer holding threats over her. Why doesn't she come home?"

Philip turned away. "Perhaps she's afraid to."

Two elderly women, one very feeble, and an extremely good-looking girl, supposing Aurora were with them, would not be an inconspicuous trio.

The search intensified when it was established beyond doubt, after visits to the Bayswater hotel and to her doctor and dentist, that the body of an old woman who had met her death at the foot of a steep and lonely cliff, having obviously been driven there in a car, was that of Blandina Paxton.

It seemed evident that at the time she had died her solicitor, who was significantly in possession of a Power of Attorney from her, had thought she was completely alone in the world. She had not seen fit to divulge to him the existence of a feckless and shaming younger sister who later, deprived of her weekly remittance of five pounds in cash, began to make very awkward enquiries.

Whether that younger sister still existed was beginning to be a matter of grave doubt.

"But now Armand is dead, nothing can happen to her!" Lydia protested.

"Not if Armand was alone in the plot. I begin to think he was only the catspaw for that super dragon."

Lydia laughed shakily.

"You're mixing your metaphors. And June's still pining for the return of the man with the key to Aurora's flat. After all, we know now that wasn't Armand. I feel that all this has the simplest explanation if only we could think of it."

"We'll have to think quickly," Philip said grimly.

"You mean Clara's in danger?"

"Not Clara, no. I don't think they'll do anything to Clara now. It would be madness."

"Then you must mean Aurora," Lydia said slowly. "Because she knows too much?"

"She's always known too much."

"But if she's in it willingly——"

"Do you think she is? Armand, being a man, might have

167

protected her, but now there's only that she-wolf, and I don't imagine she'll care any more for a young and beautiful woman than she did for the old and senile."

"There's the handsome chauffeur," Lydia said uneasily. "If he *is* the chauffeur I imagine he will have made himself scarce by now. If he isn't——"

Philip looked at her. "Are you thinking what I'm thinking? What we both should have thought long ago. That the handsome Jules may be the man with that door-key in his possession?"

Only one fact emerged in the next few hours, but that was a significant one. Blandina Paxton, a wealthy old woman living almost parsimoniously in a quiet hotel, had, in the past five years, used up the astonishing sum of nearly forty thousand pounds.

Securities had been sold, amounts had been withdrawn from her various banking accounts, all, apparently, for the purpose of re-investment in other better, but as it appeared, non-existent properties or shares.

It was as neat a piece of daylight robbery as he had come across, Sergeant Peters said.

No wonder Armand Villette had ducked out of trouble via an overdose of sleeping pills. He must have thought he was sitting pretty, a trusting, senile old woman like that, alone in the world, who had been pathetically easy to hoodwink. Although, at the end, she must have been troublesome, since it had been necessary to end her life. No doubt also she had had several predecessors. But the predecessors apparently hadn't had younger sisters, appearing so inconveniently out of the blue that a story had had to be spontaneously fabricated to prevent the police being brought in.

"They probably intended to tip Clara over a cliff, too," Sergeant Peters said. "But seeing she had this slight stroke they may have decided to be patient and wait until she had another. All nicely legitimate, as no doubt Hannah with the heart trouble was. But you two, with your poking and prying, forced their hands. And now what have we got? A suicide, and two run-away women, plus this rather anonymous bird, the chauffeur. Now that," he said thoughtfully, "is a man I'd like a word with."

Little as Philip liked Lydia staying in Aurora's flat, someone had to be there, for it was possible Aurora would try to make another telephone call.

Lydia was certain now that everything Aurora had done had been against her will. As witness the locked bedroom door, the smuggled messages in Clara's letters, the crumpled chiffon dress pushed into the back of the wardrobe in the locked room.

What was she wearing now, Lydia wondered. One of Blandina's (the false Blandina) cut-down, severe black dresses, so that no one would notice she was young and beautiful?

She insisted on staying in the flat, and then hated being alone and had to beg for June Birch's talkative company. So that there were two of them to jump when the telephone rang, or footsteps seemed to hesitate outside the door.

Usually the telephone caller was Millicent who had had to be told what was happening, and who was in a constant state of nervous panic.

Then at last Sergeant Peters rang to say laconically, "We've picked her up."

"Who?" Lydia cried. "Aurora?"

"No, the old lady. Clara Wilberforce."

21

She was having a nice strong cup of tea in the cafeteria at Victoria station. She had been there for two hours enjoying the freedom, realising how much, during those days in the country, she had missed the bustle and noise and passing faces. She loved faces. They were like leaves turning in the wind, some bright and young and shining, some crinkled and dry, some showing their undersides, their seamy, private sides that were intensely interesting to the onlooker, but careless of them, poor dears. Because one didn't show one's more distressed and uglier thoughts, Miss Wilberforce mused as she sat on the hard chair, elbows resting on the plastic-topped table.

One determinedly made the best of any situation, even of the one in which she was placed. Though that had been a great deal more pleasant since she and Blandina had been alone at the seaside.

Jules had driven them to the station early the other morning and they had taken a train to Brighton. So exciting. Though there Blandina, in spite of her wealth, had turned mean and taken only one room in a rather seedy-looking boarding-house. The beds had been uncomfortable, and she had had to lie all night listening to Blandina turning and twisting and occasionally snoring when she lay with her long nose pointing to the ceiling.

Nor had Blandina let her out of her sight during the day, although Miss Wilberforce would dearly have loved to potter down the esplanade alone and perhaps post a letter on the pier. No, it had been the old, familiar, bossy attitude.

"You know you always managed to lose yourself at the seaside as a child!" Or, "You're not strong enough to walk that far. You've had a serious illness." Or, "Didn't the doctor say no letter writing."

On the other hand it had been rather nice to have someone genuinely concerned with one's welfare, and when Blandina was not flinging out sharp orders she was very quiet. She had a plotting, planning look, and Miss Wilberforce was happy not to interrupt her in this private state of mind. It was exciting to breathe the crisp sea air and to see life going on, and to be away, if one dared admit it, from the silent midnight intruder in her room, from the noise of Jules's mower over grass that didn't need cutting, and above all from nephew Armand's generous but vaguely embarrassing attentions.

But this had lasted only for two nights and a day. Then Blandina had had an urgent telephone call. She had come back to say curtly that they were going to catch a train.

"Oh, I liked it here!" Miss Wilberforce said regretfully. "I was enjoying the sea air. It was doing me a great deal of good."

Something had upset Blandina, for her cheeks were sallow and sunken, her eyes fiercely black and gleaming.

"Where you're going next will do you more good. Oh, mon Dieu, can't you even keep pins in your hair to have a little neatness? No, you must look always like a scarecrow."

She had never spoken like a Frenchwoman before. But all at once she looked foreign, a sallow and old and bitter foreign woman.

Miss Wilberforce was frightened. She put her hand apologetically to her soft, untidy hair and explained vaguely that since her illness her hands shook so much.

Blandina quickly and roughly pulled the straying hair straight and pinned it, and said, "Put your hat and coat on. Hurry! We have to catch this train. It's very important."

"Where are we going now?" Miss Wilberforce asked timidly.

"Never you mind. But you ought to be happy. You'll be able to write as many letters as you like. Yes, I promise you that. A dozen a day if you want to."

"Goodness me, I don't know a dozen people!" Miss Wilberforce murmured, overwhelmed. "But that's very kind of you, Blandina."

The old eyes snapped at her between their wrinkled bird's lids. "Don't thank me. Thank your so dear nephew Armand, the fool!"

She said that as if she hated Armand. One had thought they were so devoted. The problem was too much for Miss Wilberforce. It had been difficult to concentrate since her illness. She really just enjoyed sitting watching people, and this she was able to do in the train for the next hour or so, and then in the cafeteria where Blandina had taken her.

"We'll have some tea," Blandina had said, and had found an unoccupied table in the corner.

But after ordering the tea she had sprung up suddenly, saying she would be back in a few minutes. Clara was to wait there for her.

171

Miss Wilberforce wondered if she were feeling ill, she had left so abruptly. But even a few minutes' respite from her overpowering presence was a pleasure, and she hadn't been too alarmed.

Fifteen minutes, then half an hour had gone by. This was too much. At last Miss Wilberforce had had to go and make enquiries at the cloakroom.

But the attendant there couldn't be sure a very tall old woman in black ("with a rather long nose," Miss Wilberforce had specified, in curious apology—she had always been troubled by the length of Blandina's nose) had come in.

"I couldn't be sure, could I, duck? You can see how many people are in and out. Regular main highway, this. But she's not here now. If she's your sister you'd better go on home and let her find you there."

"Yes. Thank you," Miss Wilberforce murmured, with her infallible politeness, and went back to the cafeteria for another cup of tea. She enjoyed sitting there in this strange freedom, and some more tea might help her to think clearly.

For it did begin to look a little as if Blandina had left her behind, like a piece of unwanted or forgotten luggage.

At last the waitress, looking kind but bewildered, said, "You can't spend the day here, dear. Which train are you waiting for?"

"I'm not waiting for a train. I'm waiting for my sister. She said she'd be back, but she hasn't come."

"How long ago, dear?"

"Oh, let me see, about two hours."

"Well, I never! Hadn't you better give up and go home?"

"But I can't do that, actually. I haven't got a home except the one Blandina is taking me to."

"Blandina! Did you say Blandina?" The girl seemed very excited.

"Yes, I did. Do you know her?"

"Not personally, dear. But all the newspapers do. A name like that. Look, love, wait there a minute. Promise not to move."

"Of course I won't move if you ask me not to," Miss Wilberforce said with dignity, and thought that the girl's face had been like a broad oak leaf, turning red in a frosty sun.

It was later that day that Lydia and Philip visited Miss Wilberforce in the hospital where she had been taken for observation and care. But she wasn't able to tell them any more than she had already told the police.

Her illness had been genuine, according to the doctor's report, she had been domineered and bullied by Blandina, but otherwise had been well cared for. She had exchanged no more than a few words with Jules, the gardener and chauffeur, although she said he had always seemed to be lurking near or in the house, and she had never seen Aurora unless she were the thin woman who had come and interfered with her drinking glass in the night.

The morning Blandina had taken her away she had thought she had heard someone crying, but Blandina had said she was imagining things.

The only thing that had seriously distressed her had been that when she had come to open her handbag in the train she had found that a great many of her letters had disappeared.

But no one was to worry, she said, smiling her gentle illumined smile. Blandina had promised she could write as many as she wished in the future.

"Did you ever think Blandina wasn't your sister?" Philip asked.

"That's what that nice policeman asked me, too. Yes, I did at first. It was that long nose. There's never been another like it in our family. But then when she was so bossy I knew it must be Blandina. I expect she's gone off again because she's ashamed of me. Not being able to keep my hair tidy and remember things. But isn't it nice that at last she's allowing me to write my own letters. I didn't like being treated like a child and told what to say."

So they were back where they had started, Philip said, with only a missing bride, and he was pretty certain she hadn't a wedding ring on her finger yet.

173

Looking at his haggard face, Lydia miserably twisted her own ringless finger. Aurora's absence, she decided, was even more effective than her presence. For this way, she haunted them completely.

22

The first thing Aurora saw when she opened her eyes was the photograph of the girl on the bedside table. The face was young, round, not particularly pretty, completely strange to her, and the girl wore an evening dress with sequined shoulder straps that had an old-fashioned look.

So the photograph was probably some years old. But whose was it, and why was it by her bedside?

She raised herself on her elbow and instantly the room swung darkly and dizzily. She felt terrible. She had missed taking tablets when they were travelling, but last night she had been forced to take them again. Jules had sat over her and there had been no escape.

So now her senses were completely blurred and she couldn't remember how she had got here, or indeed whose room in what house she was in.

A door banging downstairs made her start, and then she heard Aunt Blandina's voice declare loudly and bitterly, "It's madness, I tell you! Madness!"

Jules gave his familiar derisive laugh.

"On the contrary, it couldn't be more sane. There's food in the refrigerator, by the way. George won't mind us using it." Again he laughed. "You might get us a meal. Aurora should be awake by now. She'll be hungry."

Then his footsteps came up the stairs.

Aurora was lying tense when he appeared at the door.

"Well, darling. Awake? How do you feel?"

"Terrible! It's those pills." Her voice had developed a whine. "I don't want to take any more."

"Neither you shall in a day or two."

"Why can't I stop now?"

"Now?" He regarded her thoughtfully. "I think not, angel. I'm not quite sure——"

"Sure?"

"That I can trust you." He came to sit on the bed. "Isn't it ridiculous that I don't quite trust you?"

She evaded his smiling gaze. Her eyes went again to the photograph of the strange girl.

"Who is that?"

"Someone called Susie. Not particularly attractive, is she?"

"Then why is her photograph here?"

"Because this is—or was—her room."

Aurora started up.

"Isn't she coming back?"

"No. She's in Paris. She won't come back. Though if she does——"

"What?" Aurora asked in a whisper, because suddenly his eyes had that blank stony look again.

"If she does, it will be a pity because I will have to kill her," he said briskly. He saw her expression. "Now, don't look so outraged. I was only being funny."

"Funny!" she exclaimed. "Funny! Oh, God!" And she buried her face in the comforting pillow.

"By the way, I'll tell you something," she heard him saying. "You don't have to worry about that pendant any more. That little problem has solved itself. So long," he added inexplicably, "as Armand stays dead until I get out of the country."

I, he said. The first person singular.

The fact slowly penetrated Aurora's dulled mind. At the same time he had hold of her arms and was pulling her upright.

"But there is something I want you to do for me. Come along. Pull yourself together!"

She felt sick and dizzy as she sat upright. She couldn't remember when she had last eaten. He hadn't let her go in the restaurant car on the train. But had that been today? Or yesterday? Or last week?

175

"Come along, darling. Downstairs. I want you to ring the milkman."

"The milkman!"

"Yes. We have far too much milk. Come and see."

He helped her down the stairs and along a narrow passage to the kitchen. Aunt Blandina, tall and sombre, was beating eggs in a bowl. There were five pint bottles of milk on the table, also several unopened newspapers.

"You see?" said Jules. "We've plenty of milk for as long as we're here. And we don't want any inquisitive milkman round in the morning."

Aunt Blandina raised her bleak face. "I've told you, it's madness to stay here at all."

"Nonsense!" Jules gave his charming smile. "It's as safe as houses. We've got to eat and we've got to sleep, and also to acquire one or two necessary articles. Where else better? George won't be back."

Aurora lifted her heavy eyelids, propping them up with her fingers. "Is George Susie's husband?"

"Yes, darling."

"Has he gone to Paris, too? Does he know we're using his house?"

"Of course, darling. We're very old friends. Now, this is the milkman's number. I'll dial it for you—do buck up, for goodness' sake—then you just simply say you're Mr. Browne's secretary ringing from London, and as he's away he doesn't want any milk until further notice."

But now Aurora's head shot up with a semblance of her old alertness.

"Is this Mr. *Browne's* house?"

"Yes. I thought you knew."

"Then where is he?"

"I've told you. He's gone to Paris after his wife who, I'm sorry to say, has run off with someone else, as she's been threatening to do for years. George, as you can see, went off in such a hurry that he didn't bother about last-minute instructions to tradesmen. So we're doing him a service. Now are you going to do as I tell you?"

His eyes were stony, colourless, full of their hypnotic power. She nodded helplessly. "Tell me again—what I have to say."

It was not difficult after all. The chatty voice of the milkman at the other end of the wire told her he had been a little bothered about what to do since the Brownes didn't seem to be taking the milk in.

"Nearly got the police round," he said heartily.

Jules took the receiver from her and gently laid it down. "That's fine, darling. You did that very well. Now let's see if we can find George's passport. He must have one somewhere."

"But you said—" her eyes met his and her voice trailed away, "—he had gone to Paris," she finished lamely.

He didn't answer. He didn't intend to answer, just as he never did when her questions were awkward or unanswerable. He began making an unhurried and systematic search in drawers until suddenly he gave a satisfied exclamation.

"Here it is. Good old George. Knew he wouldn't let me down. Now that photograph—fairly simple to substitute——"

"It's too risky," came Aunt Blandina's harsh voice at the door.

"Who's complaining of risks at this stage? This is what I came here for."

"Darling," said Aurora, with a tremendous effort, "won't we want Susie's passport, too?"

"But Susie *is* in Paris, I'm afraid. She's run off. I told you."

"Then——"

"I told you not to worry about it," came his voice, suddenly edgy, showing for the first time his extreme tenseness.

Aurora stared at him unbelievingly. She still felt terrible, her head was aching and her mouth tasted dry and queer. But all at once shock had cleared her mind. She was able to think. In Jules's smiling, watchful face she saw the truth. This was where, driven into a dangerous corner, he was deserting her. The terrible old aunt, sombre and unafraid, he may be taking, or leaving to her own capable devices. But Aurora was to be sacrificed.

177

It was not the girl in the photograph, the absent Susie, who was to be killed. It was she.

In that panic-stricken moment of knowledge she acted intuitively. She turned and made a dash down the passage for the front door.

But she was clumsy from weakness. She stumbled. Anyway, he had caught her almost before she had started.

He gripped her arm in his iron-hard fingers and took her back to the kitchen.

"None of that, angel. We can't have that. Aunt Blandina is making an omelet. She's very good at omelets. She'll be deeply hurt if you don't stay to share it. Look, anyway, you're as weak as a mouse. You'll fall if I let you go. See!"

Aurora swayed dizzily against the wall. Aunt Blandina's eyes dropped to the work in hand. She began to turn the egg-beater again, the rasping noise filling the small room. Beyond the window it was growing dark. The house, situated on the edge of a field, was isolated and lonely. If anyone saw a light in the window they would only think it was George Browne because he had not mentioned that he was going to be away.

And if by any chance his wife Susie, regretting her rash behaviour, decided to return home and came walking innocently up the garden path, Jules, with his never-failing presence of mind, would ask her to share their omelet, before putting his iron fingers round her soft neck, or driving her to the edge of a cliff. . . .

Aurora wondered dully how long it would take him to make the necessary adjustment to George's passport, when the moment of goodbye would come for her. . . . She guessed that she probably had, like a condemned criminal, until morning.

They had their meal, eating Aunt Blandina's omelet, sitting at the kitchen table. Jules and the old woman, Aurora noticed incredulously, ate with good appetite. She, because they were watching her all the time, and because it was wise to eat (even though the rest of one's life was to be so short), forced herself to swallow a few mouthfuls. The food did her a great deal of good, which made her wonder how long it was since she

178

had eaten. She was able to ask quite calmly, "Where is Miss Wilberforce? What have you done with her?"

"She's perfectly safe," Jules said, and the bitterness in his voice made her believe him. He had apparently failed with Miss Wilberforce, and this was serious. "This is all your fault, you know. If you'd told me at the beginning the old woman had a sister we would have managed a great deal better. But no, you had to let that young man of yours and his girl-friend meddle. You see now why I don't trust you?"

"Stop it now, Jules," said Aunt Blandina in her curt, angry voice. "We've got to get out of here before we start recriminations. Get on the telephone and make those air bookings."

"Yes, aunt dear. At once. Keep an eye on Aurora for me. She's not to be trusted."

Of course this old woman was not Aunt Blandina, Aurora reflected. She had been called that all the time, for old Miss Wilberforce's benefit, but one knew she was someone else altogether. Because the real Blandina, that vague, lost old woman who hadn't liked the long drive, and whom one had felt so sorry for, was dead. One knew that. It was the nightmare that had been with one for weeks. So this old woman must be the real aunt. . . .

She heard Jules's voice, crisp and businesslike, "Yes, a single ticket. The name? George Browne." Presently he hung up and dialling another number made the same request for a seat on the next flight. "For Miss Honoria Chabrier," he said.

Aurora saw the briefest look of satisfaction and relief pass over the old woman's face.

"We will travel by different air lines," she said calmly.

Honoria Chabrier. So this, at last, was the famous Aunt Honoria. It was, ironically, a relief to know that one aunt did exist!

Jules came back into the room.

"You'll have to be at the airport at 7 a.m." he told her. "Air France flight leaving at seven forty-five. They'll have your ticket ready. There's a train about six. I'm afraid you'll have to walk to catch it. Pity George didn't have a car."

"And you?" the old woman asked tensely.

179

"I follow in an hour." His gaze flickered to Aurora. "Time enough," he said, and his face was deeply lined, brooding, queerly angry.

If she had still been under his spell, in that moment Aurora would have been sorry for him. Because he didn't really want to kill her. Old women who were soon to die were one thing, but this was another. The act was being forced on him, and it made him frustratedly angry, even more so that there was the night to spend first.

Or should he wait all night? Those were the thoughts behind his graven face, and now that she was no longer mesmerised by him she could understand him. It was her own fault entirely that she had shut her eyes to his cold ruthlessness for so long.

"We've got to get away from here," the old woman was muttering uneasily. "I still say we were mad to come here, in spite of getting that passport."

"Oh, shut up! Wash the dishes, and then let's get a bit of sleep. I've told you, we're safe as——"

His words were cut off by the telephone ringing.

It was like a rude intruder into their isolation, a vociferous Peeping Tom.

Jules froze. "Let it ring!" he snapped.

"But who is it? Supposing it's one of the neighbours!" The old woman's face had gone yellowish.

"Let me answer it! Let me answer it!" Aurora sobbed. Jules's hand caught her wrist. He was taking no chances. The shrill bell went on for another quarter minute. Then, with a hopeless ping, it stopped.

Aunt Honoria dropped the cup she had been holding, as if her hand had become nerveless. It smashed on the tiled floor, but its clatter brought her back to life. "We can't stay here now. I've told you all along——"

"Then go!" shouted Jules, his taut nerves snapping also. "Go and shiver all night on the railway station, and have fifty people asking questions. But Aurora and I stay here. We're safe. I've told you. Do you go rushing over to the house of every person you ring without getting an answer? Of course

180

you don't, You say they're out, and forget about it. For heaven's sake, Aunt Honoria, I counted on you keeping your senses."

"It's been—a long day," the old woman muttered. "Very well. If you stay I stay."

Jules patted her arm. "That's better. Now I suggest we put the lights out, and sit in the front room. If anyone should come we'll see them first, and we can either lie low or slip out the back way. But no one will come. Who is there to come?"

Who? Aurora wondered desperately. Not even Susie, ashamedly back from her jaunt to Paris. . . .

23

When the telephone rang and the woman's voice spoke Lydia thought it was Aurora.

She said, "Hullo!" breathlessly, and the speaker, under the same misapprehension as Lydia, went on rapidly,

"Is that you, Aurora? You remember me? I'm Joyce Walker. I took your job at Mr. Villette's office. I say, isn't it *awful* about his death? I've been in Spain for a holiday—I went after he sacked me—and I've just got back and read about it. What on *earth* happened?"

"He took sleeping pills," Lydia said automatically. "I'm not Aur——"

She was interrupted by the excited and shocked voice.

"Sleeping pills! Is that what it was? But he didn't seem the sort, did he? I mean, so good-looking and *virile*. Though I thought he was getting a bit odd. He just told me one lunch-time not to come back, he wouldn't be wanting me any more, and paid me a whole month's salary. So I went on this holiday. How is old George taking it?"

"Old George?"

"George Browne. I always called him old George. He's so

181

middle-aged, isn't he? I've been trying to ring him, but I can't get any answer."

"*Who* is George Browne?" Lydia asked tensely.

"Why, Armand's partner. I say, that *is* Aurora, isn't it?"

"Actually it isn't," Lydia confessed. "I'm her sister. I've been trying to tell you. But I'd love to know about this George Browne. Do you know where he lives?"

"Down in Surrey, just outside a village called Moston. And he doesn't get on with his wife. He used to look awfully miserable. I say, why are you so worried about him? I thought it was the handsome Armand who had taken the sleeping pills."

"So it was," said Lydia breathlessly. "At least, until five minutes ago. Look, I think I'll have to ask you to ring off. I've an awfully urgent call to make."

The constable who answered her call to the station, however, did not share her excitement.

"Sergeant Peters has gone down to the country, miss."

"When will he be back?"

"In the morning, miss. It's nearly midnight, you know."

"Yes, so it is. I'm sorry. But something important has come up in the Villette case."

"Villette? The suicide chap? Oh, yes, what information have you got?"

"Mr. Villette's secretary has just rung me. She's back from a holiday abroad and read about Armand Villette's death. She says he had a partner."

"Did you take her name and address, miss?" came the maddening prosaic voice.

"Oh, not her address. I'm sorry. But she told me about this partner, George Browne. She says he lives near Moston in Surrey."

"Moston in Surrey. George Browne. Yes, I've got that. I'll tell the sergeant in the morning. You really ought to have got that young lady's address."

"Is the morning soon enough?" Lydia cried, obsessed with her feeling of urgency.

"Houses don't run away. We can take a look at this place tomorrow if the sergeant thinks it's important, and have a word with Mr. Browne."

But they couldn't have a word with Mr. Browne, Lydia thought fatalistically. Because now she was almost sure of the truth. But it would be useless to try to make that prosaic constable who lived by facts believe her fantastic intuition.

There was only one person who would do that.

She dialled his number feverishly.

Presently a sleepy voice grunted into the receiver.

"Philip! Are you awake? This is terribly important."

He came awake at once. She could almost see it happening. "Aurora!" he shouted.

"I don't know. It might be. Can you get a car?"

"Even if I have to steal one! What is it? No, tell me when I get there."

His response was more than satisfactory. She had to crush down the jealous pain that he was flying so fast because of Aurora. This was no time to be thinking of herself.

He was there in an incredibly short time, and clattered up the stairs, careless of the noise he made.

"Moston in Surrey. No, I don't know where it is, but we'll find it. Who's there?"

"Armand's partner, George Browne, should be. But if not him, at least his wife."

"Is she going to mind us calling in the wee small hours? Well, who cares? Coming?"

"I say, what are you two up to?" demanded June Birch, sticking her be-curlered head out of her door. "Eloping?"

"Not today. Tomorrow," said Philip over his shoulder. "Sorry, June. See you when we come back."

Lydia was beside him in the car. He started the engine and they shot off with a roar.

"Now," he said, "tell me. How did you find out about George Browne, and where is he?"

"I think," said Lydia, very slowly, "I think at this moment he is waiting to be the principal figure at his own inquest."

Finally, however, they got lost. They were in the heart of the country, and everything was asleep. The last person they had asked directions of was a night porter at a railway station. After that, all the houses were in darkness, all the roads empty.

"It's three o'clock," said Philip, stopping the car. "I think at this stage we'd better wait for daylight. Are you tired?"

"Practically dead."

"Put your head on my shoulder."

Lydia obeyed, closing her heavy eyes.

"Probably that constable was right after all," she murmured. "Can you sleep, Philip?"

"I'll just have a cigarette."

"I hope we're not too far away from Mr.—I mean, Mrs. George Browne. But supposing her husband hasn't been home lately, why hasn't she been alarmed?"

"At the crack of dawn we'll find out. Go to sleep now."

And she would too, she thought, with remarkable contentment. For this may be the only time ever that her head would rest just there.

It seemed a very short time later that Philip was announcing, "Crack of dawn. There'll be someone about. Let's get moving."

He was restless, and in a hurry to move on. The brief enchantment of the darkness was over. Lydia tried to smooth her tumbled hair, and was conscious of her heart, like a stone, low in her breast.

"Where are we?"

"We'll ask at the first house. Must be approximately there. That railway porter said it was only a few miles."

The first house was a farmhouse. A burly, elderly man was clanking milk pails on the concrete strip at the back of the house.

He was the local milkman, he said, and certainly he knew the George Brownes. But it wasn't any use their calling because there was no one home. There hadn't been anyone home for a couple of days. He wouldn't have left the milk, but no one had asked him to stop it until last night.

"Who asked you then?" demanded Philip tensely.

184

"A young lady, sir. Said she was his secretary speaking from London. Go on over there if you like, but you won't find anyone home."

Philip got back into the car.

"A couple of miles," he said to Lydia. "There isn't anyone home, but we'll take a look all the same. It could be that whoever is there just doesn't like milk."

The house, a two-storey period cottage, was set in a garden behind a high privet hedge. It was in a rather isolated position, with fields running behind it down to a stream, and beyond that the railway line. Mr. George Browne apparently liked a quiet country life, with no immediate neighbours. In this, in a more modest way, he resembled his employer, Armand Villette.

The similarity between the two men's homes and habits did not stop there, for this house, like Greenhill, had a silent, deserted look. Certainly it was very early morning, and it was not likely that windows would be thrown open and people stirring. But the curtains were drawn in all the downstairs rooms, and before they walked up to the front door Lydia knew with certainty that no one would answer their knock.

"It's an awfully strange hour to call if there is anyone home," she murmured.

"It's a custom in the States to invite people to breakfast," Philip said inconsequentially, and put his finger on the bell. They could hear the sound shrilling through the house, but when it ceased there was nothing but silence.

They stood on the doorstep breathing in the exquisite early morning air full of the country fragrance of fresh grass, lime trees and the wistaria blossom on the strong, ancient creeper climbing up the front wall. It was an enchanted landscape, just as it had been in the village where Aurora's wedding had been planned. It seemed quite fantastic that there could be any undercurrent of mystery and violence.

"There isn't even a clock ticking this time," Lydia murmured. "Knock, Philip."

He pounded on the door in an unmannerly fashion, but again there was no sound from within.

185

"Let's go round to the back," he suggested, and they picked their way across the dew-soaked grass to the back door, which also stood firmly shut and secret.

"Wherever George Browne is, he's not here," Philip said at last. "We've had our trip for nothing."

"But, no!" Lydia gripped his arm. "Didn't that milkman say he had been leaving milk. Then where is it? Who has taken it in?"

"He said a woman had rung him from London," Philip said slowly. "But if the milk's gone, she's been here to move it, hasn't she?"

"She rang from here!" Lydia declared, and now she was whispering, for it seemed that after all the silent house must have ears. Listening ears, hidden furtively just inside that closed door, or behind the curtain-drawn window.

"Was she here alone?" she whispered.

Again Philip gripped her arm. His face was tense and excited.

"This is where I do my coconut palm trick again. The curtains weren't drawn across the upstairs windows. I'm going to climb up the wistaria and take a look inside."

"Oh, yes, do!"

"We can't wait all day for Sergeant Peters who goes gallivanting in the country." At the foot of the wistaria he spared time to give Lydia a quizzical glance. "You're all for this breaking and entering, aren't you?"

"I'm absolutely terrified. Can I come up, too?"

"You stay right where you are."

In no time he had reached the low top-floor windows, and was looking in.

There was one moment when his lean body seemed frozen. Then he shouted abruptly.

"Throw me up a stone. Anything. I want to smash this window."

Lydia, acting instantly, threw up her shoe. Then there was the sharp splintering of glass, and Philip's arm was inside the window undoing the catch. In a moment he had wriggled through the narrow space into the room.

186

But it seemed an eternity before the front door opened, and he stood there, grim and haggard, saying, "Come upstairs! Quickly!"

She lay there on the bed in the small, low-ceilinged room. Her dark hair was spread on the pillow, and her dark lashes rested on her white cheeks. She looked beautiful and completely remote, an ice maiden, a sleeping beauty wrapped in her centuries-long sleep.

But she was still breathing.

Philip straightened from feeling her pulse. The limp hand dropped from his.

"Where's the telephone? It's too late to try coffee, but you might make some. Don't worry about the back door. It's open. He's gone."

"Gone!" Lydia repeated stupidly. "Who?"

"Whoever was here when we were knocking. He's making for the railway, I should think. I'd like to get him, but we've got to try to save Aurora."

"Can't you wake her?"

"You try. Sleeping pills, I should think. I guess that's what he's been doing to her all the time."

The telephone was in the little sitting-room downstairs. Philip picked it up and began to dial.

"I shouldn't worry about that," said a voice behind him. "We've already picked up Armand Jules Villette. The real Armand Villette. Interesting, eh? I've been paying a visit to his country house and discovering quite a lot. Now, where's the body?"

It was Sergeant Peters. He stood there, smiling faintly.

"Been trailing you," he added. "Nice work. You flushed out the rat."

"Aurora's upstairs," said Philip tautly. "But get a doctor first. It's urgent."

She was not dead. With youth and luck on her side, the sleeping princess would open her eyes to see her kingdom again. And not, after all, a greatly changed kingdom.

Philip was still there, the old woman, Clara Wilberforce,

187

garrulous and cheerful, was still there, also Lydia, Millicent, waiting impatiently and anxiously at home, and June Birch, as golden-haired and blasé as ever.

George Browne, Armand Villette's chief clerk, kept in the background because he had been struck·off the rolls as a practising solicitor some years ago, but duly grateful to Armand for giving him a job, and unable to refuse any strange and guilty task asked of him because he was well-paid for these, and if he lost his income he might also lose his restless, extravagant, dissatisfied wife Susie, was off the scene permanently.

It was George Browne who lay quietly waiting for his own inquest. Having at last lost his adored but faithless wife, and knowing the depths of his implication in his employer's affairs, he had given up.

The man Sergeant Peters had arrested as he attempted to catch an early-morning train at Moston, his shoes wet from the long, dew-drenched grass, and a false passport in his pocket, was Armand Jules Villette. His elderly aunt, Honoria Chabrier, tough, callous, and, when caught, as venomous as a snake, was picked up at London Airport.

They were charged with the murder of Blandina Paxton, who, before she had fallen seemingly accidentally over that steep cliff on the Dorset coast, had been systematically robbed of all her wealth. There would be several similar cases in the process of investigation.

It looked as if Aurora Hawkins had been an accessory, but, with the evidence of constant drugging, in addition to the assets of her youth and beauty, she was likely to get off lightly.

The story was over. Or was it just back to where it had begun, with a wedding being arranged in an idyllically lovely English village?

Several hours later Aurora had recovered sufficiently to see Lydia.

She lay flat in the narrow hospital bed, and opening huge black eyes said faintly, "Darling, you look like something the cat brought home. Honestly!"

Lydia smoothed her tousled hair. She said apologetically, 'I've had no sleep."

"Not like me. I seem to have slept for years. Literally. Armand made me take those relaxing pills or whatever they were. Otherwise I was not to be trusted, he said." She sighed deeply. "It doesn't matter now. I've told the police everything."

"Aurora darling, are you well enough to talk? It was a—a near thing, wasn't it?"

"So I gather. Yes, I want to talk. I told you, I've been sleeping for years. But Armand made me."

"You keep saying Armand. Didn't you call him Jules?"

"Yes, sometimes. It was the name his family used. His aunts." Her voice was full of weary disillusionment. "I was madly infatuated with him. I had been ever since I started work in his office, and if he'd told me to go to the moon, I'd have had a shot at it."

"You mean, he persuaded you to help with the old lady. Blandina Paxton."

"Yes. But only to come with him when he took her to the country. I thought she really was his aunt. He'd had several —like that." Aurora's face was pinched and full of misery. "It was only after I read about the unidentified body found on the coast and added up one or two things that I guessed the truth. But I couldn't go to the police about it. I loved him too much. I just got so shocked and frightened that I decided to marry Philip, whom I'd just met, and get away. I'd make myself forget Armand."

She shivered a little.

"But I couldn't, you see. He wouldn't let me. He pursued me. I thought at first it was because he loved me. He'd given me expensive presents in the past, and he'd always said we'd get married one day. When he rang me at Millicent's that night he said we'd go to Edinburgh and be married. So after I left Philip at the other side of the village green I went and met Armand, like a fool. He was waiting in his Jaguar just round the corner. I only meant to talk to him, but he more or less kidnapped me, there and then. He said he couldn't let

189

me go about talking, in case I said too much. It was better to be married because a wife didn't have to give evidence against her husband, supposing anything went wrong. I was mesmerised by him again, if you can understand that. And I really think things would have been all right if I hadn't told him, carelessly, that the old lady Blandina Paxton had given me that pendant, because she was grateful to me for being kind. Kind! And I'd left it behind. And also I hadn't told him about the sister turning up because I was so afraid he would get her, too. So everything began to go wrong. We never did have time to get married, and after that he didn't want to. He was too busy. You had started interfering, and old Clara Wilberforce had appeared on the scene again. Armand made poor George Browne impersonate him when you came into the office that first time. George had no idea where all this was going to lead him, poor devil." Aurora sighed again, with immense weariness. "After that it was too late to do anything except try to warn Clara, and try to stop them poisoning her."

"Were they?" Lydia asked, horrified.

"I don't know. They say they weren't. She was ill, anyway. But I was scared. I used to change her glass of water at night. That was when I wasn't too sleepy and stupid. Half the time I hadn't the faintest idea of what was going on. Armand made me take those pills. You don't know what he's like when he's charming and irresistible. He used to stand over me while I made those telephone calls." She stopped. A tear rolled down her cheek. She looked white and forlorn, with the face of a prematurely old child.

"Then?" Lydia prompted.

"Then he heard about George's suicide—and it was all rather awful. He knew he had to get out of England, and he could only do it on a false passport. Because if Armand Villette lay dead, Armand Villette couldn't be catching a plane. Could he? So he took a frightful risk and went to George's cottage. And that was the end. I knew he meant to kill me, and after a while, like poor old George, I decided it would be just as easy to be dead. So I let him give me the pills. He didn't even have to force me. He was—just a little sorry."

190

Lydia took her hand. "Forget about it now. You're going to
e all right. Philip's waiting——"

Aurora opened her eyes. "Philip!"

"He saved you, you know."

"You did, too." Again she smiled, her heart-breaking attempt
t casual raillery. "My God, darling, you do look rather a mess.
)o go and put on some make-up. By the way, that nice
ergeant thinks I might be able to go home when I get out of
.ere. Do you think Millicent——"

"But she'll adore it!" Lydia cried. "She's waiting. She's on
he telephone every ten minutes."

Aurora closed her eyes.

"I'll start again," she whispered. "Truly."

When she got back to the flat Lydia, as she had promised,
mmediately rang Philip.

"She's going to be all right, Philip. She's dreadfully miser-
.ble, but she'll be all right. You'll be able to see her by to-
norrow."

"Good," said Philip briefly.

The silence became awkward. Lydia had never before been
)ereft of words with him.

"She wants to go home. Millicent is delighted. She'll pamper
.er, and Geoffrey will sulk, and everything will be the same
.t it always was." She thought of the sleepy, tree-shadowed
'illage, with the languid swans, and the church bells, and
.dded, irrelevantly, "Even the chestnut blossom won't be
ver."

"Fine," said Philip. "May I come over?"

"Here? Why?"

"I want to see you."

"Oh! I look rather ghastly. Aurora said so, too. If you
lon't mind."

"I don't mind," he said, and hung up.

Lydia sat in front of Aurora's mirror, and put rouge on her
:heeks, then rubbed it off because it looked so startlingly red.
;he was too tired to do it properly. Anyway, it didn't matter.
n a few days Aurora would have her brilliant beauty back,

191

and she, Lydia, would be just the younger sister, not particu
larly noticeable, not even particularly witty or amusing t
compensate for her lack of beauty.

She shouldn't mind. She had always been perfectly happy
that way.

But even as far back as a month ago, she had not been i
love. . . .

The door was opening behind her. "Sorry," said Philip
"Did I startle you? You're getting just like your sister, no
closing your front door properly."

Lydia put her hands to her cheeks.

"No, I'm not like Aurora," she said automatically. Then sh
tried to pull herself together. "She didn't ask for you becaus
I expect she doesn't want you to see the way she looks jus
now. But she's going to be all right. She's awake again, any
way."

"So am I," said Philip.

"But you always have been!"

"Not quite, Lydia dear. Not enough to know how mucl
more I prefer a face like this—come here, let me look at it—
yes, it isn't quite at its best, is it?" He traced the shadow
beneath her eyes, her creased forehead, the tense line of he
mouth. "It is rather the worse for wear." Sharply his voic
trembled. "But it's the kind of face I like."

And at last he had her in his arms, so tightly that for ;
moment she thought she had lost consciousness.

Then she heard his voice indignantly, "Lydia! My God
why are you crying? Now!"